THE FINAL TALES OF SHERLOCK HOLMES

(VOLUME FOUR)

By

Dr. John H. Watson, M. D.,

as edited by John A. Little

Paperback ISBN 978-1-78705-147-8
ePub ISBN 978-1-78705-148-5
PDF ISBN 978-1-78705-149-2

Published in the UK by MX Publishing
335 Princess Park Manor, Royal Drive, London, N11 3GX
www.mxpublishing.com

Cover design by Brian Belganger
http://zhahadun.wixsite.com/221b

Contents

Foreword   4

Sherlock Holmes And The Kew Gardens Gnomes   8

Sherlock Holmes And The Portobello Pornographer   39

Sherlock Holmes And The Camden Counterfeiter   69

Sherlock Holmes And The Kensington Kidnapper   111

Sherlock Holmes And The Undiscovered Country   139

Foreword.

The story of how these late adventures of Holmes and Watson came to be discovered has already been related in the first three volumes of this collection. I repeat it now for those few who may have inadvertently missed these books.

The building known to all Holmes afficionados as 221B Baker Street had fallen into such disrepair by 1955 – thanks to the efforts of the German Luftwaffe, and many years after the detecting duo had passed on – that the local authorities deemed it unfit for habitation. It had to be knocked down. By my father, as it happens.

Eneder Little had built up a successful business as a builder in London, having been forced to emigrate from Ireland after the lunatic DeValera's disastrous economic policies of the 1930s. His company (Motto: 'No Job Too Big For Little') was granted the contract to demolish nos 220A, 220B, 221A, 221B, 222A, 222B, 223A and 223B Baker Street and rebuild a terrace of spanking new luxury four-bedroomed town houses, complete with all modern conveniences.

Before the buildings were due to be levelled, he was examining the basement at 221B when he discovered a tall dust-covered office cabinet hidden in a corner behind a dilapidated kitchen dresser. Having no keys, my curious father grabbed his jemmy and cracked open the lock that controlled the four metal drawers. There was nothing but wrapping paper inside the top one, but the other three drawers revealed a series of packages of A4-sized spiral-back handwritten notebooks, each held together by two elastic bands in the shape of a cross. Never having read a book in his life apart from his annual accounts, he had no comprehension of his discovery. But he was a cautious man and decided to dump the lot into a cardboard box and take it home that night. And then promptly forgot all about them.

I became aware of this event when I was helping my mother and sister to clear out his effects the day after his funeral. He married late in life, and returned to live in Dublin towards the end of the 1970s with his wife and two small children.

I had climbed up a ladder into the attic and started handing down cartons of what was obviously rubbish – ancient account books from his building company, newspapers, magazines, old clothes, sporting equipment from his hockey and cricket-playing days – when I discovered a cardboard box, covered by some spare fibreglass insulation. Its bottom was lodged firmly between two beams and pulling it out almost caused my foot to slip off the beam and crash through the bathroom ceiling.

A rapid inventory produced sixteen packages, each of which contained a varying (one to nine) number of notebooks dated from 1925-1930. Later, when we were sitting down, exhausted after our day's work and with our shared grief, I asked my mother about them and she told me what little she could recall of their origin at 221B Baker Street. I pulled off the elastic band and opened the first notebook of a package marked February 1925, the earliest period. Intriguingly, it showed a faded red stamp with the tiny word 'Strand' repeated around the edges, and 'REJECT' in large letters diagonally across the middle. It was in surprisingly good condition, for a manuscript that had lain in its cardboard coffin for over eighty years.

I had only to finish a single chapter to realise what I held in my hand. All my life I had been a great fan of Holmes and Watson, and had read their exploits avidly, once when I was a teenager, and again when I had been hospitalised for a week while some varicose veins were being stripped. After a quick check of all the packages, it became clear that we had in our possession one novella-length and fifteen shorter adventures of the Baker Street detectives in the last years of their lives, all of which had been rejected for publication by Strand Magazine for a variety of reasons. One of them pitted the pair against the evil witch of Clapham Junction. Others treated pornography, rape and necrophilia. These were dark subjects for their time, but it occurred to me that Conan Doyle's later pre-occupation with all things supernatural – caused by the loss of his wife and son – may have been a factor in the rejection of the final detective stories, which, as everybody knows, should always have a rational solution, with no hint of smoke and mirrors, magic acts or spiritualism.

As I read on through that dark night, I understood why the first story had never been published within their lifetime. It concerned a number of quite appalling serial murders that, in the London of 1925, would most certainly have caused public mayhem and a possible breakdown of society, had it been fully reported in the press, or if Holmes and Watson had not finally solved the case. After a small amount of editing by me to smooth out Dr. Watson's archaic style, this story has been published as a separate novella within '*The Final Tales Of Sherlock Holmes – Volume One*', entitled '*Sherlock*

Holmes And The Musical Murders'. The first five shorter stories followed in '*The Final Tales Of Sherlock Holmes – Volume Two'*. The next five continued in '*The Final Tales Of Sherlock Holmes – Volume Three'*. Volume Four, which I trust you are about to read, contains the last selection of the final tales, also suitably edited.

John A. Little,
Portobello,
Dublin,
Ireland.
March 31st, 2017.

12.   Sherlock Holmes And The Kew Gardens Gnomes.

Now that the end is nigh, so to speak, I wish to commit to paper one of the last cases Holmes and I worked on together. This horrific affair occurred during the appalling winter of 1928, a very difficult period in the lives of the residents at 221B Baker Street.

Although the great Thames flood in January had not encroached upon our higher ground in the district of Marylebone, it happened that Lily Hudson's mother, sister of the formidable Martha from our earlier years together, was unfortunate enough to be staying with an old friend in Bankside, and had been swirled away by the deluge, never to be found. An atmosphere of gloom descended upon our household throughout the rest of January and February, which sent Holmes reaching for his needle, and myself, of course, for the bottle. After all, what would old age be like without an occasional injection of cocaine hydrochloride and a tumbler of the drop that cheers?

Especially if you are suffering from an incurable disease and have been given only a few years to live, methinks.

Our discomfort had been exacerbated by the continuing illness suffered by Lily's baby and my beloved godchild, young Sherlock George Lestrade, who had spent the first seven months of his fragile existence vacillating between death's door and life's black pram. I had diagnosed diphtheria and was treating the sickly mite with a toxoid, mixed with a dose of aluminium salts. Happily, by the middle of March, when this nasty tale first entered our lives, he was beginning to show signs of improvement, and no longer spent all his waking hours struggling for breath. He had even begun to smile at me.

Whereas I doted on the lad, and took every opportunity to look after him for Lily and Jasper, Holmes simply refused to have anything to do with his namesake. Indeed, when the screams from downstairs became too much for him to bear, he took to wearing his wireless headphones to shut out the din. Apart from looking ridiculous, this had the frustrating effect of preventing those casual conversations I valued so highly in our relationship. It was like living with a profoundly deaf person, who kept asking me to repeat whatever reply I had made to one of his penetrating comments on some Times article:

'Eh, what's that, Watson? What did you say?'

This was usually followed by an awkward plucking of the headgear by about a centimetre above his ears.

It was while he was trying my patience in such an irritating manner, late one Saturday evening in March, that we first became aware of the Kew Gardens Gnomes, and their roles in a number of arsons.

As with many of our later cases, it was initiated by the sound of our young housekeeper's boots clumping up the stairs. But before Lily had sufficient time to introduce him, our faithful Baker Street Irregular, Wiggins, the only one of those dozen street Arabs to avoid prison in later life and now a strapping middle-aged man, had burst past her, and literally thrown himself at the feet of the startled detective, sobbing violently.

'They is gone, Mr 'Olmes! They is all gone!' he cried.

To give him some credit, Holmes removed his headphones and bent down to grab his former retainer by the lapels of his threadbare jacket.

'Who do you mean, man? Exactly who has gone?' he demanded.

Wiggins dragged his sleeve across his nose, relieving it of an impressive stream of emerald snot.

'My 'hole family,' he groaned. 'My lovely wife, Marjorie, and my three little girls. All ... gone. All ... dead. All ... blackened and shrivelled up!'

He gazed around at me with wide red-rimmed eyes, as though I had been personally responsible for his loss. I managed to hobble across, place my arms around his broad shoulder, and help him gently up onto the rattan sofa.

'There, there, old chap,' I said. 'Now why don't you settle yourself down and tell us all about it? You have obviously experienced an enormous shock. What on earth has happened?'

Wiggins sat down abruptly and placed his head in his hands while I poured a decent slug of medicinal brandy for him. Having downed it in one gulp, the grief-stricken fellow shuddered, pulled a gargantuan handkerchief from inside his jacket and proceeded to blow his nose vociferously into it. When that noisy action was completed, he wiped his eyes with the back of his hand, scratched his muttonchop whiskers in agitation, and made a heroic attempt to speak rationally.

'As yer knows, Mr 'Olmes, I works down at the docks as a lifter. Often I stays late, for the extra money, like. It were only ... about a couple of 'ours ago that I 'ad finished up and left for 'ome. But when I enters my street, wot does I find, but our 'ouse ... our 'ome ... ablaze! Completely! Gone up in smoke! In smitereens!'

'A fire?' enquired Holmes. 'Most interesting. Whereabouts, might I ask?'

He had raised himself from his prone position and started to fill his briar-wood pipe from the spanking new Persian slipper, a present from me for his recent seventy-fourth birthday. The old one had simply disintegrated into tiny shreds, having provided almost fifty years of sterling service.

'I lives in one of them old Victorian cottages down in 'ackbridge. We shares wiv my brother and his family, but they was all away in Bournemout' on 'oliday, a merciful blessing for them. It started in the basement and went up through the building like a dose of salts. One whoosh, and all my loved ones are gone up to 'eaven. And me left all alone down 'ere. Oh, God Almighty!'

Wiggins had started to weep uncontrollably again.

'You do realise they probably suffocated from smoke inhalation first, rather than being burned to death, don't you?' queried Holmes. If this was my colleague's attempt at sympathy with his former employee, it seemed a singularly poor choice of words to me. And to Lily, who left the room abruptly, muttering away to herself about 'soich a callus, 'ard-'earted 'tec!'

'Was there nothing that the Fire Brigade could do, old chap?' I asked.

'Oh, Doctor, they was too late. Too late. Too bloody late. Too la ...' Wiggins voice trailed off as he sunk his head into his hands yet again.

'And why have you come here?' demanded Holmes.

I was about to object in the strongest terms to the great detective's total lack of empathy when Wiggins nodded violently and answered the question himself.

'Because t'were murder, Mr 'Olmes! Murder, pure and simple. Four times over. The Chief Fireman told me so 'isself. There were a distinct odour of petroleum in the basement. Who would do such a fing? Eh? Who would want to kill my poor little family?'

Our old Baker Street Irregular gazed at us both in wonder. I am not entirely sure that he knew who we were at that particular moment.

'Who, indeed?' muttered Holmes.

'So I finks to myself, who does I know wot solves murders, and ...'

'You thought of us,' I interrupted. 'Of course you did. Quite right, too. We will be only too glad to help you, won't we, Holmes?'

My friend checked his fob. At last he seemed to have woken up to the reality of a possible crime to solve, after a tedious hiatus of seven months since the awkward adventure of the Clapham witch. And that there was a fellow human being who needed his assistance, of course. Someone who had been a great help to us in his youth, as the titular head of the Irregulars, and in more recent years as a sole agent.

'We shall do what we can, Wiggins,' he said. 'There is little point in examining the scene of these crimes tonight, especially if the Fire Brigade are in the process of corrupting it in their customary manner. You must spend the night here, in my room. The good doctor will give you something to help you sleep. I shall pass the hours of darkness thinking about this case, as I have indexed many notes upon the subject of arson. Then in the morning we shall start our investigation by involving young Lestrade from downstairs in a discussion about any enemies you may have brushed up against during your lifetime. Watson?'

I came down to table the following morning to find Holmes, Lestrade and a much recovered Wiggins tucking into one of Lily Hudson's more elaborate breakings of a fast that featured rashers of bacon, scrambled eggs, devilled kidneys, smoked kippers and a huge basket of toast and muffins. She obviously felt great sympathy for our bereaved client, although she had no idea about our past association, when he was a mere scalliwag, living shoeless and wild on the streets of London with his gang of ruffians, and helping out the two 'tecs for a shilling per day plus expenses, with a guinea prize for a vital clue.

Despite the baby's healthy screams from downstairs, Holmes had foresworn his headgear, possibly out of respect to Wiggins and his great loss.

'Watson. So good of you to join us,' smiled the great detective munching away on a piece of dry toast. 'Young Lestrade has a spot of news on the arson front.'

Jasper Lestrade nodded his ferret face gravely in my direction.

'Indeed, doctor. It appears that poor Mr Wiggins was not the only person to lose his house last night. There were three other instances of house burnings around London, all of them activated by some sort of bomb, thrown through a window in each case. Two of them involved no further loss of life, as the people managed to escape each time. But a complete family of seven were killed in the third fire, a grandmother, mother, father and four small children. Name of Johnson. Similar traces of an explosive device were found in each burned-out wreckage, suggesting a common purpose. The fires overlapped in time, so more than one criminal must be involved. And there were no witnesses to any of these foul abominations.'

'It is apparent that we must find some connections between the victims,' said Holmes, as he sipped his coffee. 'Motive is normally the problem in cases of arson. Obviously there is no material gain, unless someone sets their own property on fire in order to get the insurance, which I am certain is not the case here. Another possibility is revenge. It is a great pity young Wiggins cannot provide us with a single person who might have wished to harm him or his family. He seems to have led a thoroughly blameless life.'

Our bereaved client simply nodded his head in puzzled agreement. He looked to me like a man still in a state of profound shock, who would need careful attention for some time to come.

'Perhaps Wiggins can continue to stay here until he has recovered, or has found somewhere else to stay?' I suggested. 'You and I might take it in turns to use the sofa at night?'

'Splendid notion, Watson!' agreed my colleague. He had clearly injected himself during the night, just to keep going without sleep.

'Eh, many thanks for your excellent kindness, gentlemen,' intervened Wiggins, raising up a pair of eyes that looked to me like the dead ashes of yet another fire. 'But I must speak about this to my brother and 'is family. They be returning later today. They 'ave also lost their 'ome, and there will be arrangements to be made. Funerals and suchlike. We 'ave another brother, who is a builder, and in a more fortunate position than us, with a large 'ouse over in Spitalfields. I am sure 'e will 'elp us out.'

'Equally splendid! Come on then, Watson! Lestrade and I are about to examine the burned out houses.'

Holmes had sprung up from his chair in an alarming manner.

'But ... but ...,' I spluttered. 'I have not yet had my breakfast!' In point of fact I was just transferring a particularly succulent slice of bacon onto my plate.

'Nonsense, Watson! You ate yesterday, did you not?'

'Yes. And I am bloody well going to eat today also!' I stated firmly, continuing to fill my platter. 'You two can manage perfectly well without this jaded old crock. Fill me in later on your progress. I shall remain here with Charlie, and help him out with the arrangements for the ... funerals.'

'Oh, very well! Come along, Jasper! Let us away to the crime scenes!'

And that was exactly how the long day passed. After a satisfying breakfast, I worked with Wiggins in organising the tragic burial of his entire family. There was also the church service to arrange – he was a devout Roman Catholic, which came as a small surprise to me – relatives to contact, newspapers to be informed, refreshments for the mourners, etc., etc., I encouraged him to make as many telephone calls as he liked, and kept a close eye on his mental condition. Being occupied seemed to lift his spirits, and when his wealthy brother called for him mid-afternoon, I was satisfied he would cope with the difficult days ahead. I waved him off into the gathering fog with a supply of sleeping draughts, and a promise that he should contact me if there was anything else I could do for him.

I then passed a pleasant couple of hours playing jack-in-the-can with young Sherlock George, using a pencil, a rubber clown's head and a small cardboard box I had put together. His squeals of delight warmed my heart at the time, but afterwards, as I was lighting my first pipe of the evening upstairs, I became quite nostalgic for my lost wives, and fell to deeply regretting the absence of our own progeny. You would imagine that lady luck might have shone upon at least one of my two marriages. But it was not to be. There would be no young Watsons to mourn my passing. That was the sad state Holmes found me in when he waltzed into the sitting room at six-thirty, his cape and trousers seamed with smut and grime.

'There you are, Watson!' he chimed. 'Do cheer up! It doesn't do to spend too much time thinking about what might have been. There is no point in dwelling on the past and the lack of children to keep you in your final years. Dinner is on its way! It smells like chicken potpie with potato dumplings. One of your favourites, is it not?'

'Oh, yes. Of course. Good Lord, Holmes! Was it that obvious?'

Holmes proceeded to overlay page after page of the Times Newspaper into a large square on the floor and empty a bag of sooty rubbish into its centre. My nostrils were immediately assaulted by a strong odour of petroleum.

'When I perceive young Sherlock playing quietly with some game or other as I enter the building, I assume that his godfather has been entertaining him for part of the day. Then the presence of death, your own losses, your wounds and obvious melancholy ... well, it is hardly worth mentioning. You know my methods. Has our unfortunate old lieutenant, Wiggins left?'

'Yes,' I yawned in reply. 'What have you got there?'

'Clues, Watson. A veritable treasure trove of clues! Gathered with much painful groping around in the filthy ashes of the four crime scenes, with Lestrade's permission. Here. Have a look at this. What is it?'

Holmes handed me the top of some kind of colourful ornament. It looked as though it had been decapitated from some gewgaw, which I recognised immediately through the dirt.

'A decorative figurine of a gnome,' I replied. 'The pointy red hat and part of the head. Mary and I used to have a ceramic one in our back garden. He sported a fluffy white beard and smoked a cherrywood pipe while hanging out a rod to catch a passing trout.'

'Well done, Watson! I can almost picture the fellow. And the damn thing stinks of petroleum. I suppose a hollow one *could* be used as some kind of improvised incendiary device, if added to gunpowder and alcohol. There are similar bits to be found in all four sites. Now, if only we could find out where they came from?'

Holmes left the question hanging in the air. I think he expected me to come up with an answer.

'Eh, we bought ours in a shop in Richmond, I think. But I am certain they are available for sale all over London.'

'Or they may have been stolen from someone's back garden,' suggested the great detective. 'Hang on. Here's another bit. It might be a foot. And there are letters beneath it.'

Holmes leaned across, grabbed the hearth brush and proceeded to flick it delicately back and forth across the tiny mould.

'K. Definitely a K. Followed by ... damn .... it's unreadable. Then the final letter is a clear W. Kew. Kew Gardens, in other words.'

'Which is in Richmond!' I exclaimed.

'Excellent! Tomorrow we shall travel over there and check their sales lists for the past year. What else do we have?' asked my friend, as he used the handle of the hearth brush to fiddle about with the smudged debris. He picked out a small round item and held it up to the light between his fingers.

'That looks like a pebble to me,' I suggested.

'And a pellet to me,' muttered the great detective. 'But then I would think that, wouldn't I?'

'Speaking as someone whose body has been pierced by at least two Jezail bullets, I can confirm it is merely ... a stone ball,' I responded.

Holmes placed the object between his teeth and bit down hard upon it.

'You may be right, old chap', he confessed, grunting in pain.

'They might have been used to smash in the windows, before the culprits flung in their gnomic bombs?' I suggested.

'Perhaps,' mused Holmes, polishing the orb on the sleeve of his coat. 'No, wait. I know what this is. Yes. See! There are the colours. It is a ... marble! A child's marble!'

'Which may have nothing whatsoever to do with the crimes,' I said.

'Indeed. But would there not be more than one on the floor of each house, if it were a part of some child's game?'

Holmes turned his attention back to the pile.

'Now what have we here, I wonder? How did this little fellow avoid obliteration by the flames?'

He was holding up what looked to my tired eyes like the distinctive cone from a coniferous tree. Its scales looked badly burned at the edges, but the shape was still recognisable. The nostrils on Holmes' hawklike features flared with interest as he sniffed it.

'Most interesting,' he muttered after a while, putting it to one side, and continuing to delve into his pile of dirt.

More interesting to me was the sound of Lily's clogs upon the stairs.

'Why not leave it until after dinner?' I suggested, knowing full well that he would not even be aware of food until he had fully processed his find.

'You go ahead, old chap. I'll be with you in a minute.'

Oh, yes. A minute. His *minute* turned into an entire evening, followed by the night itself. And he was still there the following morning when I came down early for breakfast, albeit lying fast asleep upon the floor, headphones attached, arms and legs akimbo, beside the scattered remnants of his grimey discoveries. It took yet another minute to yank off his earplugs and wake him up.

'Watson! What time is it?' he muttered. His face looked pale and lined, his eyes like dark puddles trapped in the gutter of a street.

'Breakfast time,' I answered. 'Followed by bathing time, dressing time and going out to Kew Gardens time. Did you discover any more clues?'

I sat down at the table, hoping he might follow my example.

'Not really. Just a few other bits and pieces. The most relevant of which is a sliver from a piece of pink rubber. It has a small hole in it, and I surmise that it may have once been part of a child's catapult. We need to find out more about the victims, to establish some connection between those four families, the Simpsons, Johnsons, Armstrongs and Wigginses.'

He stood up, stretched his arms wide, strode out of the room to the stairhead, leaned over and yelled, 'Lestrade!'

Jasper Lestrade came dancing up the stairs two at a time, as though he had been summoned by Lord God Almighty himself. Which, in a way, he had.

'Yes, Mr Holmes?' he enquired.

'What do the victims have in common, Lestrade? That is the question!'

'There is nothing we have discovered as yet. Neither do the locations have any kind of link.'

'Why don't you join us for breakfast?' I suggested.

'I cannot,' Jasper replied somberly. 'I am expected downstairs. Little Sherlock must also be fed. And he does not tolerate any form of delay!'

'Have you found out absolutely *nothing* at all?' demanded my colleague belligerently.

'Believe me, Mr Holmes, we have been fully occupied in examining the crime scenes and identifying the eleven bodies accurately, as they were burned so badly. Unfortunately most of the seven children involved have no dental records as yet. However, there is some good news. Not *all* of Mr Wiggins's children have been killed in the fire.'

'Are you telling us one of his girls might have escaped with her life?' I asked. It would be little consolation to the poor fellow, but something to provide a shred of hope for the future.

'Yes. It is possible one of the three smaller bodies belongs to the arsonist himself. It was positioned well away from the other corpses.'

'A male child?' queried Holmes, pausing in his efforts to squeeze a pipe cleaner through the stem of his clay.

'Yes.'

'Pyromaniac children? Now that *is* interesting. I don't believe there is a documented case of such crimes before. Exactly how do you know this?' continued my colleague, setting fire to his atrocious plugs and dottles from the previous day.

'The body length indicates a more mature child, say about thirteen. Wiggins's three girls are four, six and eight years of age.'

'And can *he* be identified by his teeth?' asked Holmes.

'No. We do not have centralised dental records for criminals as yet, although there is talk of such at the Yard. And there were no fingerprints at the crime scene, of course,' replied Lestrade. 'Be assured that we will be focussing our attention on discovering who this lad was. It won't be easy, as children of his age go missing all the time in London, and are never reported. Most of them are either orphans, or they want to get away from an abusive environment at home. They might have been abandoned by their feckless parents. Especially if the family is from a lower class. Boys in particular tend to form gangs and live on the streets, if they can't get work as sweeps or mudlarks.'

'But *where* is the missing girl?' I demanded impatiently. 'And does Wiggins know that she lives?'

'Of course. The eldest girl, Fiona, was staying with a friend when the fire occurred. She was reunited with her father last night. But the shock of losing her mother and two sisters ... ?'

'Indeed,' mused Holmes, puffing so hard on his revolting farrago that I could not see his head through the halo of acrid tobacco smoke. 'It will be difficult. The problem with juvenile criminals is, they can be hard to find. Being so small, they can hide anywhere. It is obviously a gang, which has lost one of its members.'

'But surely some of the other three arsonists might be adults?' I conjectured. Why not?

'Possibly, Watson. Possibly. But considering the clues, I doubt it. Now. Your favourite subject. Food. Followed by a slow brougham to Kew Gardens, and a spot of gnome-hunting!'

My charming physician had given me the bad news in November of the previous year. 'The words "liver" and "cancer" should never appear together in the same sentence,' he had muttered, as though this expression of his final judgement might mollify me. Having a little experience of medicine myself, I had already guessed the truth.

'It has probably spread from your colon. There is no way of knowing. Too many pipes, and far too much brandy down the years would not have helped. As a doctor, you should have known better. Surgery can be of little assistance in either case. But with your advanced years, progress of the disease will be slow. Plenty of morphine for when the pain becomes too great. Anything between one and three years. Will forward the bill to you. You can see yourself out. Goodbye.'

I had told noone, not even Holmes. Oh, he knew I was ill, right enough, but I had gone to considerable lengths to persuade him that my agony was caused by those famous wounds from the ancient battle of Maiwand, still niggling away at my shoulder and leg after so many years. Do not our injuries come back to haunt us later on? The last thing

I wanted was to be thought of as a helpless invalid by my best friend in the whole world. Especially when there were still dastardly crimes to be solved and foul villains to be hunted down!

Now, as our cab trundled across the streets of London towards Kew Gardens, I was struck by the irony in my doctor's words. *Morphine for the pain.* Perhaps I could steal some from Holmes' supply when the need arose?

But of course I had not reckoned upon the great detective's abductive ability, wherein he used existing facts to generate an hypothesis about unknown events. Not for the first time.

'How long?' he asked.

'How long ... what?' I replied testily.

'How long have you got, Watson? Unless that blasted Maiwand wound of yours has mysteriously travelled from your leg upwards to your inner organs, which you keep fondling protectively, and your recent mood swings have something to do with the absence of females in your life, which I doubt, your continuing weight loss and yellowish features tells me that you have a serious disease of, I suspect, the liver.'

'Two to three years,' I sighed.

'Excellent!' he cried.

'Just *what* is so damned good about it?' I demanded.

'Well! To know how long you have got to live! What a gift! Think of the benefits! You can plan a budget and we can dine out in all the best restaurants in London whenever we want! Until the end, that is. And having lived *quite* a good life, you will be joining your two wives in heaven, or so you appear to believe. You will experience no more physical pain. No more awful nightmares about those wars you fought for the benefit of your country, wherein you were often chased up and down the Khyber Pass by a herd of angry elephants. Don't worry, your loud moans have echoed down the stairs throughout many a night. Besides. You are seventy-five now, with some added months, if I remember correctly. You will probably be in your seventy-ninth year of life when you die. While your body is deteriorating, your brain is still functioning at its proper level, and you will be able to help me out in my important work during your last days. Really, the time between eighty and one hundred are best avoided, old fellow. Twenty years of scratching your head, trying to remember your name and worrying about the location of the nearest toilet. It is not worth the candle. Oh, no, thank you. The first sign of mental confusion that assaults me, will lead to an immediate overdose of cocaine, and I shall be joining you in your precious summerland. But who is to say that I shall not reach the spiritualist heaven before you anyway?'

I slumped back disconsolately into my carriage seat. If this jabbering represented Holmes' attempt at cheering me up, it did not work. I had always known that my friend lacked any form of feeling for his fellow humans, but I also supposed that news of my impending demise might have elicited from him some small degree of regret, or commiseration. For instance. Would he not miss my company just a little bit? For an hour or two? Oh, well. At least he wasn't patronizing me and treating me as an invalid.

'Here, let me help you,' he offered, as the carriage came to a halt outside the Victoria Gate entrance to Kew Gardens.

'Just ... bloody well leave me alone!' I protested, stepping onto the pavement. Unaided, except for my blasted stick!

It was a surprise to me, but obviously not to Holmes, to discover that neither plant nor book shop existed at the Royal Botanical Gardens, selling recognisable gnome figures that could be broken up and used as makeshift bombs to burn families to death.

'The entire area of Richmond was severely flooded in January. As you can see, the gardens have not yet recovered fully. Be careful with your stick, old chap. The going may be slippery. We shall walk along this path around the outskirts. There should be a commercial premises open somewhere.'

The morning fog was lifting as we circled slowly, enjoying the sounds of children playing in the bushes, and nodding at happy couples and nannies with their prams strolling in the opposite direction. The magnolia trees were in their final blossom, with petals drifting down as we progressed along our route. Eventually, after passing under a ruined arch, we came upon a sad-looking tea-room, which appeared to be in the process of opening up for the day. A hefty woman of indeterminate age with grey hair tied up by a garish scarf was sweeping out the entrance.

'It'll be another hour or so before we start up,' she grunted at us.

'We just want to know if you sell any gnome figures,' replied my friend.

'Or where we might buy some around here?' I added.

She paused, leaned against her sweeping brush and glared at us as though we were a couple of lunatics.

'Even if we did sell them, which we don't, why bother to spend good money on something you can easily steal?' she suggested, not without a trace of sarcasm.

'But we are not thieves!' I retorted strongly.

'Where can we find these unguarded gnomes?' asked Holmes.

'Where all the other bloody thieves find them! Just look around you! We've lost about ten over the last few weeks, along with a cat, two fairies, and three bullfrogs! There's a very fancy garden out there somewhere, full of stolen Kew ornaments! Now go away and let me get on with my bloody work.'

We took our hurried leave of this obstreperous female, and headed along a grassy tree-lined path towards the impressive Pagoda, keeping our eyes open for further examples of the gnomic figures as we pottered along. A hazy sun appeared in the distance beyond the Chinese folly to add some warmth to the day and cause a choir of joyous robins to serenade us from within the bushes.

'Ten octagonal stories, Watson, each of which diminishes by one foot in diameter and one foot in height, as they taper towards the sky. Such mathematical exactitude pleases my sense of symmetry enormously. Did you know the Chinese used to build an underground palace beneath their Pagodas, to house relics and other funerary objects?'

'No.'

And he was the one who didn't like cluttering up his mind with useless information!

'I wonder if the architect, Sir William Chambers, included such a room here, underneath the base platform? Such a damn pity the thing is not open to the public.'

'I thought we came here to look for gnomes,' I muttered, still annoyed at his apparent lack of interest in my medical condition. And that cursed Afghan reward was beginning to give me gyp again.

'Patience, old fellow. Let us take a closer look at this extraordinary structure.'

'You go right ahead. I shall take the weight off my feet upon this bench.'

Holmes whipped out his ever-present magnifying glass and approached the door to the Pagoda, while I eased my aching body down onto the seat.

Away from the public paths, Kew Gardens seemed blissfully peaceful, the only sounds being a faint rustling within the bushes to accompany the birdsong. As I sometimes do when I am tired, I fell into a kind of dozing daydream, wherein my mind flicked nostalgically through an internal album of cases and people from the distant past – dancing men, orange pips, red heads, speckled bands (snakes), stains, pince-nez, crooked men, Mrs Hudson, Mycroft, Lestrade, the Baker Street Irregulars. The Baker Street Irregulars. The Kew Gardens Gnomes. *The Baker Street Irregulars.* Suddenly I was wide awake, standing up, shaking my stick and shouting at my associate across the path.

'Holmes? I say, Holmes!'

He gestured at me to be quiet and turned his attention back to the base of the Pagoda.

But I would not be silenced.

'Wasn't one of the original Baker Street Irregulars called Simpson?' I yelled.

Holmes stared across at me as though I had become the ghostly manifestation of his ancient enemy, Professor Moriarty himself. Then his eyes went up to heaven and he actually clapped his hands to his head. After that he ran over and hugged me in a manner that caused me quite a bit of anguish and seemed far too familiar to me.

'I say, old chap,' I ejaculated. 'Steady on!'

'Beg pardon, Watson. Yet again you are the stormy petrel of crime. You see? Your mind still lives! That is the connection. Some young street arab named Simpson helped us out in your bloated tale of ... what was the damn thing called?'

'The Crooked Man!' I cried.

'Yes! A tragic case! But this means there will be more fires to come, I fear. How stupid of me! Of course. Oh, of course!'

With this enigmatic repetition, he entered the familiar trancelike state that usually indicated a high degree of furious ratiocination. A frisson of the old excitement crept up my spine.

'Eh, it might just be a coincidence?' I suggested.

'What? Simpson and Wiggins? Oh, no. We were not aware of the full names of all those Baker Street lads, but I am sure the four families whose houses were burned out, will prove to have helped a certain consulting detective to solve several mysteries in their childhood. I sensed from the beginning that this case was all about revenge. No, not *revenge*. That is too personal a word. *Vengeance* is more like it. Justice for past crimes. And I do not believe our friend Wiggins is being entirely truthful about claiming to have no enemies.'

'But maybe he was just too overcome by events. What would any of us be like if we had just lost our family?'

'Who knows? We must speak with him again. He can tell us the names of all twelve of the original Irregulars, most of whom spent some time in prison in their adult years. I wonder why? What were their crimes? Are any of them still behind bars? And how many were returned to society, got married, and created a family? All questions to be answered back at Baker Street later on today.'

'Yes, but what about the gnomes?' I asked irritably. All we needed to do was find one of the blasted things and prove that they were the source of the bombs. I felt suddenly exhausted. I had seen quite enough foliage for one day.

Holmes stared over my shoulder into the bushes.

'The gnomes?' he grimaced. 'Why, it would seem that they are right behind you.'

Holmes' revolver appeared to have replaced the glass in his hand by some form of magic. I turned around slowly, assuming that he was playing some unpleasant trick on me. Unfortunately, he was not.

The three ragamuffins each held one of the garden gnome figures in their hands, poised and ready to be thrown at us. Their faces were so filthy and pinched that I could not be certain they were actually young boys. I thought of dwarves. They snarled at us as though we were dangerous vermin, their faces so full of loathing that I raised my stick at them.

'Stop!' shouted Holmes. 'Put down those bombs immediately or I will shoot! I warn you! My Colt has a hair trigger!'

It is an obvious fact that this story would never have been told if they had thrown the makeshift bombs at us, hit their targets, and the great detective and myself had been set ablaze, to share an agonising death being burned alive in the Kew Gardens.

In truth, the hair trigger on Holmes' gun saved our lives. Although he denies it to this day, I firmly believe that his shot was accidental. It was pure chance that it hit the branch of an overhanging black locust tree, which snapped and fell upon the trio of desperadoes, causing them to panic, drop their gnomic bombs and rush away from the ensuing flames, which engulfed the same tree and reduced it to a mound of grey ashes. But did not, thank heavens, do any damage to either my friend or myself.

Later on that evening, over well-deserved brandies and cigars, Holmes and Lestrade recounted the events of the remainder of the day to me. After the gunshot, this pathetic invalid had been dispatched to Baker Street to fetch the young detective and his Scotland Yard team, while Holmes chased after the arsonists.

'I knew exactly where they were heading,' he said, blowing concentric smoke rings ceilingwards. He held up the blackened cone between the tips of his forefinger and thumb. 'This is the fruit of the *sequoiadendron giganteum*, or giant redwood. The thought had occurred to me when I perceived how difficult it would be to climb the Pagoda, even with its gradually reducing levels. So I went directly to the Redwood Grove, and managed to catch sight of the last pair of legs scrambling up into one of the trees. I was then able to mount guard until you arrived with your men, Jasper.'

'Do you mean to tell me that three young lads were living up a tree in Kew Gardens!' I protested.

'Young arsonists, Watson. And there were *four* of them, not three. Two of whom have succeeded in killing ten people! And two of whom have tried, and failed to do the same thing. Let us not forget the deeds of the remaining three. Or their destinies in Borstal Prison until they are old enough to pay the proper price for their crimes. Yes. By all accounts, and I am relying upon the evidence of one of the more athletic constables that arrived over there, they had constructed a perfectly comfortable tree house which was invisible to the park keeper, or to any passing stranger.'

'And had been living there for several months, during the winter,' murmured Lestrade.

'So they were homeless. But why did they try to attack us? And why on earth were they setting fire to those houses in the first place?' I asked.

Holmes leaned forward and poked the fire vigorously, sending a shower of orange sparks shooting up the chimney.

'I should have realised sooner that the motivation for these crimes was rooted in the details of what happened to the Baker Street Irregulars later on in their lives. Not for the first time, Watson, you set me upon the straight and narrow. Because there were twelve of them originally, I expected more fires to be started. Today the ringleader of the feral gang, named Freddy Murphy, once he had calmed down and given in to his fate, made the following statement to Scotland Yard and myself under close examination. Read it out again for Watson's benefit, Jasper.'

Lestrade pulled out several sheets of paper from within his jacket and settled his cigar upon an ashtray.

'The lad could barely speak the Queen's English, so I have interpreted and translated what he said to the best of my ability, as well as rearranging the details into a more coherent story for the benefit of the court, when his trial finally comes about:

"My name is Frederick James Murphy. I am fourteen years of age, and of no fixed abode. I had a happy home once upon a time, up until my eighth birthday, but on that very day my father murdered my mother and my two little brothers with a hatchet in a drunken rage. This hurt me bad inside, but I was able to hide under the staircase at the time, and so I survived, to escape later. He was hanged eventually, but as a pauper and orphan I was taken away immediately to live at the workhouse in ...

'Oh, my good lord,' I groaned.

'Hush, Watson,' Holmes admonished.

'... Poplar. I stuck the continual beatings and other things going on in that place for two years, then ran away to the city and lived on the streets, foraging and begging for food. At night, I'd find somewhere nice and dry and quiet, like under a bridge or a hedge in a garden or park. It was better than the poorhouse, except when it was cold in winter. I was left alone and I did okay, being a small boy with not too bad manners. Over the next few years, I met up with the other three lads, who were in a similar position, and we formed a kind of gang. But pickings were getting poor for us beggars, and we had to start thieving for our food. We were good at that too, and soon we had progressed to separating grannies from their handbags, pickpocketing, and even holding up old codgers in their shops. We each had our own knives by then. About six months ago, we decided to find somewhere warmer to live during the winter, and I had the bright idea of building a house up one of them big trees in Kew Gardens. It wasn't that difficult, as we were all good climbers. We nicked the wood, hammer and

nails from a builder's yard, and worked at night in the park when there was nobody around. It only took us a week or two, and then we would sleep there each night, shin down at dawn and grab a lift into London on a lorry for the day's pickings. Then home again after dark, to sit around for a few smokes and tell each other stories before we went to sleep. One night, my pal Nicky ... "

'He was the one who immolated himself at Wiggins' house,' interrupted Holmes. 'He must have followed his gnome through the window when it failed to go off, and then dropped it by accident and been caught up in the conflagration.'

"... told us a story that hit me very hard, being as I was still missing my mother and brothers a great deal. It went some way to explaining my dad's boozing and killing. On his deathbed, Nicky's father had told him the truth about his childhood membership of a certain gang, and given him a list of the eight people who had subsequently led him into a life of addiction, which caused the breakup of his family, and subsequently, Nicky's own life on the streets, as his mother had died giving birth to him, and he was an only child.

I had always remembered the fondness with which my father talked about his childhood, (when he was off the booze,) especially his time as one of a bunch of lads called the Baker Street Irregulars, who helped out this pair of famous detectives, Sherlock Holmes and Doctor Watson, the same two that we followed to Kew Gardens this morning. Their house was on our list, you see, and we were checking it out for subsequent gnome-bombing, Nicky himself having disappeared somewhere during the night."

'At this stage of the interview, I informed Murphy of the demise of his cohort Nicholas Joyce, and it was some time before the tough little brute was ready to speak again,' commented Lestrade brusquely.

"Nicky told me that his father was also a member of the same group of lads, and that such an experience had been of great importance in his childhood too. It was shortly after their services were no longer required, as the main detective had lost interest in solving crimes and wanted to keep bees or wasps or beetles or some other insects down in the country, that things started to go badly wrong in both our dads' lives. All of the Irregulars missed the excitement of being trainee detectives, if you like, so they decided to continue operating as unofficial crime-fighters. The gang even changed their name to the Baker Street Regulars, with Wiggins still the boss. They kept their wits about them, and soon the rozzers in the Yard had started to rely on them for information about all sorts of suspicious shenanigans. Small payments were again made for their work. But there was one copper who really hated them, and would not believe anything they said, out of pure jealousy for the assistance they had provided earlier to Sherlock Holmes. He swore that he would put a stop to their amateur sleuthing, even if it meant the end of his own career. His name was Lestrade."

'My father was not inclined to listen to anybody. As you know yourselves all too well, gentlemen,' smiled Jasper weakly.

Holmes waved his pipe around in a vaguely forgiving gesture. I merely nodded my head in agreement. More ghosts from the past!

"He did his best to disband the Regulars, by spreading dirty lies about them around Scotland Yard, one of which was that they were making up the information they were peddling. This had the effect of reducing the number of Regulars who were interested in fighting crime to just four, including Nicky's father and my own. Each of the other eight members decided to turn to a more profitable life of crime, again led by Wiggins. And so the Baker Street Regulars became a different type of gang, burgling houses, robbing banks and pushing drugs, mainly cocaine ..."

'But surely cocaine was a legal substance in those days,' interrupted Holmes. 'And still is, to my knowledge.'

'Absolutely not,' I stated firmly. 'It was banned under the 1920 Illegal Drug Use Act, as I have mentioned to you on several occasions recently. It leads only to physical and moral decadence. Before 1920 it was only available in pharmacies by doctor's prescription, so there would have been a thriving and profitable black market for it.'

My friend appeared to shrink visibly into his chair.

"... while the remaining four continued to help Scotland Yard with their enquiries. One day, the criminal eight were trapped down at the docks while transporting a huge shipload of coco leaves, in preparation for the production of cocaine from them. By that same Lestrade copper, as it happens. They were prosecuted for running drugs, and sentenced to ten years each in His Majesty's Pentonville Prison. But in return for his own freedom, Wiggins made a deal with Scotland Yard to implicate the other four innocent lads by planting coco leaves in their homes, and they were also picked up and received the

same sentence. So Lestrade had put away eleven of the original Baker Street Irregulars. Three better than eight. Cocaine was in plentiful supply inside Pentonville, and while Nicky's dad and mine were in that prison, at the instigation of the seven criminal Regulars, they both developed a drug habit which they could never break. When they were finally released on parole, six years later, they were but shadows of their former selves, who then added alcohol to their addictions."

'He must have been out of his mind on something, to kill his poor wife and two children with an axe,' I suggested.

'That would have been much later,' said Lestrade. 'But then consistent use of cocaine is known to have a cumulatively damaging effect upon the brain. Especially when combined with alcohol.'

'What? Cocaine? Damage to the brain? Are you quite sure of your facts, Jasper?' chuckled Holmes.

Needless to say, George Lestrade's son knew nothing about my colleague's lifelong habit.

"Nicky showed me the list of those eight Regulars who had destroyed our fathers' lives. And thereby ours, of course. Having found out where they lived, we decided to punish the eight families by setting fire to their homes. The other two lads were game for anything, and we took an oath in our shared blood to use this method of gaining a form of vengeance. Nicky's father had been in the Army, and taught him the rudiments of making a bomb with ordinary petrol. I came up with the idea of stealing hollow gnomes and fairies from the gardens and using them as containers for the fuel, with the heads broken off to temporarily hold down the cloth soaked in kerosene. We planned to use our catapults with marbles to break

the windows and then throw the bombs inside. Last night we were finally ready to start our work. It is an awful pity to me that the first half of our task did not succeed fully. I am not sorry for what we did, and am prepared to take full responsibility for my own actions, even if it means the rope. This life has been but a nasty bane to me, and leaving it early will cause me little grief."

'And that completes the lad's statement,' said Lestrade, folding the sheets and placing them back inside his jacket pocket.

'So much for Wiggins not having any enemies in his past,' muttered Holmes.

'He has surely paid a heavy price for his dishonesty. But I still don't understand why they were planning to burn down 221B Baker Street, and attack a pair of tired old detectives,' I sighed.

'They knew I was living here,' replied Lestrade. 'My father was blamed for his role in the downfall of the crime-fighting Regulars, and so I was a target. You are both famous, and the trio recognised you this morning, followed you to Kew Gardens, possibly on the back of your brougham, and used their stash of weaponry to attack the only people who might have scuppered their remaining plans. Fortunately for us, and the other four families, Mr Holmes' marksmanship saved the day.'

'Harrummpph!' I grunted.

'What did you say, Doctor?' enquired Lestrade.

'Oh, nothing.'

'Well, gentlemen. I think I hear Lily's footsteps on the stairs, so I shall bid you both good night.'

After Lestrade had left, and before I retired to my bed, Holmes kneeled down on the carpet in front of my chair and placed his hand tenderly upon my shoulder. I shifted uncomfortably, prepared for some scathing criticism of my attitude to his shooting abilities, or his continuing illegal use of cocaine.

'Watson. You grumpy old soldier. I know you think of me as a callous, unfeeling chap, without human emotions. And a decadent drug addict to boot, whose brain is rapidly deteriorating. Maybe I am both those things. But I promise you this. When the end approaches, I shall be the one to take care of you,' he said, his intense grey eyes penetrating mine. 'Nobody else. You have my word upon it.'

Well!

It was the best that I could hope for.

I suppose.

13.   Sherlock Holmes And The Portobello Pornographer.

'Must you, Holmes?' I grumbled. 'I have a really stinking headache.'

My friend, swanning around our sitting room in his mousey bathrobe, continued his vain attempt at Wagner's appalling Träume for violin, as though I had not uttered a single word. Music is supposed to soothe the soul, is it not? To my mind his melancholy wailings resembled the caterwauling of a tomcat on heat, about to be attacked by a slavering Baskerville hound. Despite his monograph about the polyphonic motets of the Franco-Flemish composer Roland de Lassus all those years ago, he really was a terrible musician. And getting worse with time! If Wagner were still alive, he would surely turn in his grave.

I reached for his wireless headphones to drown out the cacophony.

The drug treatment for my terminal cancer had many nasty side effects, one of which was an occasional excruciating migraine. Normally I would simply retire to my darkened bedroom, but I had been spending so much time there recently that I had felt the need for company. Presumably his hand would tire eventually and we might resume a conversation on some subject of mutual interest, such as the dearth of crimes in London.

That stifling summer of 1928 was finally starting to cool and bow down to the inevitability of autumn. I had just celebrated my seventy-sixth birthday, if that is the right word for an occasion marking one year less to go before the completion of my death sentence, which had been a cheery 'two to three years at most' from my blasted doctor the previous winter. Cancer of the colon, that had spread to the liver. Holmes had promised to look after me in my final days, but as he had not mentioned the subject since the case of the Kew Gardens Gnomes six months earlier, I guessed that he had forgotten all about it. Far be it for me to remind the great detective of such an arduous undertaking. Meanwhile his own constitution was as strong as ever, although he remained bored stiff with the lack of suitable cases to sink his mental teeth into.

After what seemed like several hours to me, but was probably only twenty minutes, Holmes finally ceased his abominable scraping. He placed his Stradivarius gently upon the back of the sofa, reached for his music satchel, upended it, and watched gleefully as the sheets poured onto the carpet. I removed my headphones, only to discover that he was humming that same awful Wagner tune.

'Tra-la-la-ra-tra-ra-la ... Let us see what we have here,' he muttered, sitting down on the floor in the lotus position and riffling through the papers. I guessed he was looking for another piece to pluck away at. Sighing loudly, I prepared to cover my ears again.

'Hmmm. Mozart's Violin Sonata No. 21. Too difficult. Haydn's Violin Concerto in G Major. Too long. And too difficult. Beethoven's Kreutzer Sonata. Oh, most definitely not. What have we got here? Not music, but art. In point of fact, a photograph,' he declared, holding up a glossy square of paper to the light, and turning it around. 'A Kodak picture. Dated October 20th, 1927. Goodness me! How chilly.'

His glass lens appeared by magic from the pocket of his robe and he proceeded to examine the print in close detail.

'Most interesting. I had no idea they had so much ... hair.'

'What on earth do you mean by that?' I demanded.

By way of explanation, he handed it over to me.

'Good God, Holmes!' I exclaimed. 'This is a photograph of a partially naked woman leaning back against a tree, and she is showing off her nether regions! For all the world to see! While wearing high heels and stockings up to her knees! How disgusting!'

'If you say so, old friend,' replied Holmes demurely.

'Really. This is just too much! How could any member of the fair sex allow herself to be exposed in such a m-m-manner?' I stammered.

Holmes shrugged. Suddenly those grey eyes narrowed and his brow gained several extra deep furrows.

'Watson. Again you excel! Ever logical, ever valiant. That is exactly the question I should be asking,' he muttered. 'Here. Return it to me.'

I was only too glad to oblige. There was a lot I did not understand about the world of London in the late 1920s. If this was an example of it, well then I would be happy enough to say a fond farewell to such a devilish den of iniquity!

There followed yet another detailed scrutiny of the offending black and white snapshot, combined with bouts of sniffing and even a spot of licking. This went on for so long that I began to be suspicious of his motive.

'Do not worry, old chap,' he murmured. 'I am deriving no gratuitous pleasure from this exercise. None at all. As you know, I possess no animal instincts, being a mere brain. My body's sole function is to house that mind. It is clear to me from her face that this poor woman is being forced into this pose, and maybe into other, even worse, acts.'

'Presumably she is a prostitute, who is exposing herself for money?' I suggested. Who else would do such a thing? And what would my beloved wives Mary and Bea have made of such a photo, had they been granted enough years of life to see it? Pah! I would not have permitted them to sully their minds by viewing it!

'Judging by the refinement of her delicate features and those pleading eyes, I doubt it very much. Also note that one leg is considerably shorter and thinner than the other, and its knee is slightly twisted. This lady is disabled. Possibly polio.'

'I will take your word for it,' I grunted. 'Although I have no idea why you are still so interested in such a filthy picture. Which was taken almost ten months ago, I might add.'

Holmes put down the photo and reached for his Persian slipper. Before replying to me, he filled and lit his briar and puffed contentedly in my direction.

'You bought me that old music satchel for my seventy-fourth birthday last January, Watson. And a splendid gift it was, too. You had obviously noted my disorganised sheets over in the corner of this room. Where did you get it, might I enquire?'

'At the Portobello flea market,' I replied defensively. 'They have some quite good stuff down there. It is not all rubbish.'

'And would you remember from whom you bought it?'

'Yes, I believe so. His name is Barry Armstrong. He has a perfectly respectable stall, mainly leather goods. Some he makes himself in his shop, the rest he buys from dealers. Although this one was a bit faded and stained, it had been hand-stitched, with genuine leather. Rather expensive, too.'

'I am sure it was,' replied Holmes patiently. 'Presumably you conducted a thorough search of its contents before giving it to me?'

'Well, I did have a *look* inside,' I muttered. 'But I cannot be absolutely sure that bloody picture was not there in January. If that's what you are asking me.'

'Indeed. I would like to find out where this photo came from originally. There is more to it than meets the eye. And a young lady here who might need your help, old chap. Even after ten months. Are you feeling well enough to undertake a trip over there? Bring your Webley, and keep it handy. You never know what we might find.'

As usual, my friend knew exactly which buttons to press in order to motivate me. A damsel in distress. Although I still felt like I had drunk several bottles of brandy the previous night, and I found that photograph deeply offensive, I agreed to hobble across to the Portobello Road with him. I thought it might clear my head for a while. And it would certainly be better than listening to another bout of bloody Wagner.

As it turned out, my old war wound started acting up and I was unable to walk the full distance, so we were forced to hail one of those horrible motorised Beardmore taxicabs – growlers having all but disappeared from the streets during the summer – which left us off at the corner of Blenheim Crescent. This was just a stone's throw from the flea market and close to the area known as 'Little Israel' or 'Jew's Island', to which many of the wealthier jews had relocated from Whitechapel over the previous decade. The damned rattletrap had left me feeling somewhat shaky, so it took a while for us to arrive at

Portobello Road, having wended our way through a phalanx of screaming children, still on their Summer holidays and playing vicious games of conkers, leapfrog and Simon Says.

'His stall is over there,' I said, gesturing towards the one at the end of a line of similarly ramshackle stands. It was covered with many different types of leather and calfskin goods, including sandals, handbags, belts, clothes, wallets, place mats. And satchels, of course. The owner was leaning against his stall, smoking a cheroot and chatting away to his next-door neighbour, whom I happened to know was involved in selling batches of performing fleas to circuses from her barrow.

'Very well,' muttered Holmes. 'Just let me do the talking.'

I was only too happy to let him interrogate someone who had managed to sell me a music satchel which contained a filthy pornographic picture of some unfortunate disabled woman.

'Mr. Armstrong, I presume?' said the great detective, like an explorer in the jungles of Tanganyika. He had tapped his cane rather rudely upon the man's shoulder to gain his attention.

'That's me, right enough. What can I do for you, sir?' said Barry Armstrong, flinging away his cigar as he turned around. The tradesman's honest, bluff features were tanned by constant exposure to the sun. The prospect of a sale appeared to obviate any annoyance he may have felt at my associate's mode of address.

'Assuming that you did not make it yourself, you can tell me where you purchased *this* item,' replied Holmes, holding up the music satchel.

Armstrong lifted a pince-nez from within his shirt pocket and clipped it delicately onto his hooked nose.

'May I?' he enquired.

After Holmes handed him the satchel, the pedlar examined it closely, turning it around and opening it out.

'Aye, you're right. It is obviously not one of my own making,' he said.

'You sold it to me in January this year,' I volunteered.

He gazed at me over his pince-nez and a look of instant recognition passed across his features.

'Ah! I remember you now,' he exclaimed. 'A medical man, looking for a present for some musician's birthday. I gave you this at a bargain price.'

'And can you also remember from where you purchased it?' repeated Holmes patiently.

'Lordy, no. I shall have to take a peek at my Sales Diary for that. Come inside, why don't you? Beila, keep an eye on things for me!'

Armstrong led us into his studio behind the stall. The interior resembled a workshop, with a sturdy deal table in the centre containing equipment for stretching and manipulating leather, and great strips of raw skins hanging from the brick-lined walls. He slapped the satchel down on a desk in the corner, picked up a purple ledger, wet his finger and started flicking through it.

'Let me see ... November, December, January. Any idea of the exact date?'

'Some time in the week before January 6th,' I answered.

'The week before ... oh, right enough, here we are. January 3rd. One music satchel sold to a Doctor Watson. Eh, why do you want to know where I got it?' He scratched his greying stubble in what looked to me like a slightly embarrassed manner.

'We found something in it that we wish to return to the original owner,' remarked Holmes innocently.

'Right. Well, you might find such an act rather difficult, as it appears that I purchased it in early November of last year from the lead violinist with the London Symphony Orchestra, a Miss Jesenia Marple, who retired before Christmas due to ill health, and passed away only last month. An elderly lady, she was a regular visitor to the Portobello flea market, even when she was sick, and I was sad to read of her death. She was often in poor straits financially, and I bought several items from her over time, just to help her out.'

'I see. Good man. No question of turning a profit, then?' queried Holmes cynically. His grey eyes scanned the studio, coming to rest on a battered, pale green metal filing cabinet in the opposite corner. He strode across and picked up a small wooden box from its top.

'Great heavens!' he exclaimed. 'A Kodak Film Tank and camera, with all the various bits and bobs. So *very* modern. Development can take place in daylight. No darkroom needed. I have never seen one of these before. You must be quite the amateur photographer!'

Armstrong hurried over to his side.

'Eh, I use that to take pictures of the products I am selling. The ones that don't fit on the stall outside, that is. Also I advertise my more expensive items in the daily newspapers.'

'Do you mind if I take a closer look at your photographic apparatus?' asked my friend.

Without waiting for a reply, Holmes pulled out his pocket-glass and examined the box and its associated kit.

'Could anyone else have access to this camera?' he enquired, after a short while.

'Absolutely not!' exclaimed Armstrong, running his hand through his oily hair. 'Noone comes in here when I am not around. I keep the shop well locked, even when I have to spend a penny. But I am not the only one in Portobello Road that has one of these. I know of at least four other traders who use them. Some do it for business. Others take pictures as a hobby. Oh, do be careful. It is quite ... fragile. No, wait. Wait! Don't open it, please! There is a film inside! It is not finished!'

Holmes ignored the man's pleas, removing the acetate and holding it up against the light from the shop entrance. He proceeded to roll it upwards from his left to his right hand, examining each frame until he came to an obvious end.

'That will cost you two shillings and six pence for half a roll of film destroyed,' demanded Armstrong.

'Watson, pay the man.'

I obeyed my friend's instruction.

'Could it also have taken this, perhaps?' asked Holmes abruptly, whipping out the photo of the disabled woman and holding it up close to the trader's face.

Barry Armstrong's features registered such shock at seeing the filthy picture, that I found it hard to believe he could have seen it before, let alone taken it.

'I ... I don't understand,' he spluttered. 'Why are you showing me this ... this obscenity!'

'Because that is what we found inside *your* music satchel!' I burst out.

'Well, *I* certainly did not put it there! And it was not there when I received it from Miss Marple, either. I always check out my resale items thoroughly.'

'Very well,' said Holmes. 'In that case it would appear someone must have placed it in your satchel after you received it, and before or after you sold it to the good doctor. It is merely a coincidence that you possess the necessary equipment to create such a picture. Tell me. Do you recognise the lady in question?'

Armstrong flinched.

'I will have to look at it again,' he muttered.

Holmes handed him the photo. His face reddened as he perused its contents.

'No. I have never seen her before in my life,' he stated firmly. 'Gentlemen, I have no idea how such a monstrous thing should find its way into your music satchel. All I can do is repeat that I had nothing whatsoever to do with it!'

'What about the location?' insisted Holmes. 'Can you identify where the photo was taken? Look closely at the apple tree she is leaning back against, the sundial to her left, and the discarded sofa to her right, with the horsehair stuffing leaking out of it. The tree might be part of a bigger orchard.'

Armstrong was forced to examine the picture a third time. I did not blame him for not appreciating the background at first, as I had failed to notice those details myself.

He shook his head abruptly before handing it back.

'Somebody's garden, obviously. But I don't know where. Or a farm, maybe. Have you finished? I need to get back to work outside.'

'Can you tell us who the other photographers are, before we part company?' asked Holmes. 'Which stalls they own?'

'Certainly. Just let me write down the four names and trades for you.'

'I would like to know why Armstrong seemed a little embarrassed when he realised where he had purchased the satchel,' I mused, once we were outside, and heading down the road to the first stand on the list.

'Is it not obvious, Watson?' replied Holmes. 'He had been checking his Sales Diary and noted the difference between his purchase price and his sales price. He was concerned lest we became aware of the vast profit he had made out of you, old chap. Bargain price, my foot.'

'Oh. Good Lord. I suppose you are right, as usual. It seems so obvious now you mention it.' At least he had not told me that I had seen, but I had not observed!

'You see, but you do not observe. Well, what do you think? Is our friend telling the truth?'

'I believe so,' I replied, feeling more disappointed than annoyed.

'I am not so sure,' he countered. 'The coincidence is too great. I am not convinced he checks out each of his products so thoroughly. I think he scarcely looks at them, concentrating his mind upon a suitable price with which to fleece his customers. Yet his film contains nothing but a bewildering array of snapshots that feature fancy leather goods. Ah, would you have a Vesta on you, by any chance?'

We paused while Holmes set fire to his pipe. His hawklike eyes narrowed fiercely above the flaming bowl as he used this delay to scrutinize the street ahead. I had spent enough years in his company to realise that he had made some progress in Armstrong's shop, although he would be loathe to speak about it yet. His rejoinder would likely be: *It is a capital mistake to theorize before one has data. Insensibly one begins to twist facts to suit theories, instead of theories to suit facts.* Or some such ratiocination.

'This street is chock-a-block with minor villains, Watson,' he murmured, as he inhaled his tobacco with satisfaction. 'People buying goods at low prices and selling them on at a huge profit to innocent buyers like your good self. We would need a very large motor-bus to round them all up. Obviously, anyone could have placed the photo in the music satchel on Armstrong's stall when he was not looking. I fear that we are making a wasted journey, unless we can hit gold with one of these others.'

But we did not hit gold with the four vendors. Neither gold, nor silver, nor tin or even copper. None of them recognised the woman in the photograph, and all were equally outraged by its filthy contents. One lady threatened to call the police on us, which caused the great detective considerable amusement.

'It is not funny, Holmes!' I protested. 'Some of these people actually seem to think we are trying to sell this photo to them. That one of us is a ... a pornographer!'

'Well, it is certainly not me,' he retaliated. 'Come on, old chap, before you blow an entire gasket, let us head up to the Duke Of Wellington public house for a pint of ale and a ploughman's lunch. We can review the situation there.'

'An excellent idea,' I concurred.

After a decent meal, with his cherrywood pipe lit and fizzing well, Holmes leant back in his seat and proceeded to summarise our progress, or rather lack of it, to date.

'As we cannot discover who placed the photograph in the satchel, the only two clues that remain are the setting and the lady herself. It would be like looking for a needle in a haystack to find that exact garden with the tree, sundial and sofa. All we know is that it was a cloudy day, as there is no shadow on the sundial. But Watson, you are a doctor and a twice-married man who knows a lot more about the mysteries of womenfolk than I do. They are your department, so to speak. I am sure you have delivered many an infant into the world. What can you tell me about her that might help? Forget about the reason for those exposed private parts for a minute, just get a hold of yourself and go with your gut instinct.'

He handed me the damn picture again. I kept it close to my chest so that noone else could see it. To control my disgust, I had to pretend that I was examining a live patient, as I had done so many times in the past.

'Oh, very well,' I sighed. 'You mentioned the hair. Let us begin with that. Pubic hair on a woman has a specific purpose. That is to protect the genital area from dirt, bacteria and viruses. It also makes the physical movements involved in conjugal activity more comfortable for both parties, by easing friction. Judging by the width of her vulva and the vaginal opening, I would suggest she has had one, and possibly more, children. Her face is that of a middle-aged woman, perhaps forty-five or so, who may be experiencing the change of life. No doubt you will have noticed the absence of any wedding ring on the fourth finger of her left hand. Yet there remains the outline of a previous band. This could mean that she is divorced, separated or just removing it for the purposes of the photograph. The necklace would support the theory of a previous husband or lover. Her clothes are not shabby, as would be those of an ordinary tart. They actually seem quite expensive to me. She is wearing a flapper cloche hat with sequins that is popular among the women of today, suggesting she is trying to look younger than her age. The rolled up s-bend corset that can be seen briefly is an additional vanity, although many women do wear them nowadays. The frilly blouse, lace collar and pleated skirt are also *très chic*. Her silk stockings are patterned in an art deco style, thigh high and held up by ornate garter belts with clip type holds. Very sophisticated indeed. Single strap alligator shoes are really for evening wear, not appropriate for someone who is posing in a garden during the day. If she is a prostitute, as I suspect, then she is a very high class one. And although her face does seem to be pleading, that does not necessarily mean she is in trouble of any kind. There could be many reasons for it. She might be in love with the cameraman, who has just ended their relationship. Or maybe she is cold, and wants the session to finish as soon as possible. It is October, after all, and she is exposed. But we are not mind readers. Who can tell what she is thinking?'

With those words of wisdom, and feeling rather pleased with myself, I handed the photo back to Holmes. He stared at me, flabbergasted. His pipe was stuck in mid-air, halfway between his hand and a mouth that hovered like a mackerel gobbling plankton.

'Bravo, Watson! I am impressed. You really do know your stuff where the opposite sex is concerned. Such detail. So you think we are off on a wild goose chase?'

'I don't know, Holmes,' I replied. 'There does not appear to have been any sort of crime.'

'Yet I remain convinced that there is,' he stated emphatically. His pocket lens had come out again, and he would insist on holding the damn photo up for the world to see as he examined it.

'Despite your interesting monologue, you have missed all of the most important points of interest about this lady, which may have a bearing upon her predicament. That she is a smoker is obvious from the stained fingers. Not for her the *très chic* filtered cigarette holder. The skin lesion on the left side of the neck below the angle of the jaw tells us that she is also a musician, probably a violinist, but possibly a violist. It is known as fiddler's neck and is common among professional instrumentalists. As Jesenia Marple was the lead violinist with the London Symphony Orchestra, it would not be too much of a stretch of the imagination to assume they knew each other through this association. Miss Marple may even have been the photographer in this case. Or her captor, if she has been kidnapped, as I believe. Which raises the question as to where she is now? Is she also dead? Your observations about her clothes are irrelevant, as she may be wearing them just for the picture. They tell us nothing about who she is. Closer examination of the legs suggests an alternative to polio, possibly an accident that resulted in a reduction of the length of the fibula or tibia bones. Or even a birth defect. Now for the face. She is clearly of Jewish origin, judging by the fullness of the lips, the size of her nostrils and that typical aquiline nose. As, indeed, is your friend Barry Armstrong. I am sure you noticed the Star Of David emblem on the wall inside his workshop. We cannot tell the colour of those pleading eyes, but the size of the dilated pupils could mean that she has a drug habit, either opium or cannabis. The slight indentations on either side of the nose shows that she is astigmatic, and uses reading glasses. Her fine, dark, unmarked skin indicates an ancestry from the Southern hemisphere, possibly South Amer ... .'

'Right! All right!' I interrupted, thoroughly nettled at his usual parlour game. It was all I could do to avoid pouring the dregs of my beer over his complacent features. 'So why don't we just find out what has happened to this *person* from the London Symphony Orchestra, and then return to the comfort of our rooms at 221B Baker Street. My leg is bloody well killing me, believe it or not this terminal cancer is getting me down *just* a little bit, and I would not say no to an injection of opium myself.'

Holmes tented his fingertips together and gazed at me benignly from beneath those hooded eyes of his. He remained silent as my blood gradually ceased to throb inside my head and my even temper began to slowly restore itself. Then he placed a hand in his pocket and withdrew a small glass container, which he offered to me.

'Take one of these,' he said. 'It will ease the pain.'

'What are they?' I asked suspiciously.

'Morphine.'

'But these are tablets. You normally take your drug by injection.'

'Not any more. I also have a doctor, who has recommended that I no longer use needles. My tired veins and skin can take no more puncturing, apparently.'

I shook one of the capsules onto the palm of my hand and washed it down with the remainder of my beer. What the hell. When one is faced with the end of days, being a little reckless can be quite ... energising.

'Right. Where do we go from here?' I demanded, once the morphine had kicked in.

'Little Israel,' replied Holmes. 'Is it not another suspicious coincidence that our photogenic friend looks Jewish, and this area is just down the road from Armstrong's shop? Eh, Watson?'

'Perhaps,' I replied. 'But please do not show that damned photograph to everyone we meet.'

It being a Monday, the Jewish quarter was teeming with shoppers. Unlike Portobello Market, the shops themselves did not spill out onto the street. Customers had to form orderly queues outside the three poultry and butcher's shops that I noticed. It was the same for the bakeries, groceries, chemists, drapers, jewellers, watchmakers and the single boot shop.

Holmes came up with the simple idea of cutting the photograph in two, so that the offending part would not be seen by anyone in Little Israel. He showed the top half of the picture to each of the proprietors and to any of their customers who showed an interest, but without any luck until we arrived at the footwear store.

The first thing I noticed was a pair of the exact same alligator shoes that were worn by the lady in the dirty photo. They looked second-hand. I said nothing, as Holmes was busy showing the lady's likeness to a slight, balding, pock-marked young man with enormous ears, who was dressed in a black apron and held a hammer in his right hand. A light brogue was positioned upon a metal last and a set of silver nails were spread evenly across his teeth. I experienced a faint twinge of recognition, as though that face might have once belonged to some character from our distant past.

'Have you ever seen this woman?' enquired my friend. 'We need to establish her whereabouts, as she has been left a substantial sum of money in a colleague's will. She is a musician, who plays the violin.'

The young man shook his head emphatically, before removing the nails from his mouth, one at a time, and placing them delicately upon the counter.

'Oh, no, sir. She does not play the violin. Nicole plays the viola.'

'Nicole? So you know her?' demanded Holmes.

'I should do,' he replied. 'She is one of my many aunts, sir. Although I have not seen her for quite a while.'

'I see. And what is your name?' enquired the great detective.

'I'm Samuel Bosanquet, sir. It is the family name.'

'Why have you not seen her in so long?' I asked.

'I don't know. She grew up with my grandfather and grandmother across in Kensington Park Road, close to the synagogue, whereas I live in the house behind this shop with my mother and father. Thinking about it, she made no appearance last Christmas, which was unusual for her. But I'm sure she will be pleased to have come into money.'

'Christmas? So your family is not Jewish, then?' I stated. Ooops. A Holmes mistake? Surely not? Norbury, anybody?

'Oh, no. Christian. Anglican Church. You see, this shop has been in our family since well before the influx of immigrant jews over the last decade. We have never moved as they are good neighbours and customers. They may haggle a bit about prices, but we are well used to that, and take account of it.'

'Presumably your grandfather would know where she is?' said Holmes, tapping his fingers along the counter.

'He might. Eh, the poor old devil has become a bit of a recluse in recent years. Despite having eight daughters, including my mother and Nicole, noone seems to visit him any more, and mum has barred me from entering his house. He lives there with an old housekeeper.'

'What number is this house?'

'204 Kensington Park Road.'

'Thank you for your help, young Samuel. We may be back later on. Come along, Watson. The trail is getting warmer.'

Number 204 Kensington Park Road was one of an imposing line of white stucco Georgian townhouses, each with a central entrance surmounted by an elaborate portico. Unlike its neighbours, all of the front windows were shuttered, and it was no surprise to me when Holmes' repeated pressing of his cane upon the bell received no response.

'We shall have to go around the back,' he muttered.

'Oh, dear, I hope we are not going to break into yet another house. I am not sure I wish to end my days in a prison cell.'

But I was speaking to myself, as Holmes had already shoved open a splintered side door, and I found myself limping after him down a gloomy narrow passage that looked to me like something out of an early work by Mr Charles Dickens. I would not have been surprised to be assaulted by Fagin or the Artful Dodger, jumping out from behind the overgrown curtain of ivy hanging down from the side wall, ready to pick our pockets.

A postern was refusing to yield to the shoulder of my friend.

'Knit your hands together, Watson.'

'I'm too old and far too ... sick for this sort of behaviour,' I grunted, as he lifted his left leg onto my manmade platform, and vaulted over the wall like a young thing and into what I presumed to be a garden of some sort.

Holmes rattled a bolt on the far side of the wooden door for a minute or so, before edging it back against the weeds between the stone crevices, allowing enough width for me to join him. Despite the wildness of its growth, I recognised it immediately. There was no orchard, after all. Just a single apple tree, a dilapidated sofa and a sundial. But no sign whatsoever of dear old Auntie Nicole.

'Progress,' whispered Holmes. 'Now for the house itself.'

'My dear chap!' I objected. 'Breaking and entering is still a crime in London!'

Too late. He had already used his cane to smash in one of the eight panes of a mullioned window on the ground floor. Then he placed his hand carefully into the ensuing gap and twisted a latch. The window yielded to his efforts, and he was inside the house before I had time to mutter the words – *Not guilty, Your Honour*. With considerable difficulty, I was again forced to follow him through the aperture and risk a joint incarceration, rather than have to visit him in solitary confinement.

'Holmes!' I whispered. 'It is not too late to turn back.'

But he was gone. Gone to explore the basement, which yielded ... nothing. It was entirely empty. I staggered after him up the circular stairs to the first floor, which proved to be ... equally empty. Similarly for the second and third floors. Just a plethora of dusty cobwebbed rooms with furniture covered by ghostly white sheets and a musty smell of death. If it had not been in the middle of the afternoon, with daylight gleaming through the transparent curtains, we would have had no idea where we were. Our stealthy footsteps echoed through the empty house.

'Holmes, there is noone here,' I whispered. 'Can we please go home now?'

This was met by an urgent, silencing finger to his lips as we climbed up the final staircase to the wide balustrade landing on the topmost floor. Three doors led off it to ... what? More spiders and cobwebs?

Holmes patted his pocket, which I took as a gesture to remove my revolver, and to be ready for anything. Then he opened the first door. A strong light shone from within, revealing an elderly lady knitting by an empty fireplace in a comfortable sitting room. Rather like our own, actually. Sitting with her back to the landing, she did not seem to be aware of us, so after a fleeting inspection that showed a tiny kitchen in one corner and a double bed in another, my friend pulled the door to, and moved on to the next one. What we found there will remain with me until the end of my days, even though such time has been limited by my dreadful disease.

It was pitch black at first. Only when our eyes adjusted to the light coming into the room from the windows behind us, did the shadowy outline of an open coffin become apparent. We moved towards it and peered inside.

She was clearly dead. I had seen enough bodies prepared for burial in my time to recognise a corpse when I saw one. And she was less fully clothed now than when she had been photographed, being entirely naked, her knee still twisted, and one leg still shorter than the other. We were too late, if Holmes had imagined that we could save her.

As the windowless chamber gradually brightened, I noticed several sinks to one side, together with photographic plates and other bits of apparatus I did not recognise. To the rear of the room there was a bath. Along the other side a line of black-and-white prints hung pegged to a piece of string, like the washing on a line. Clearly, the room was also being used for the development of photographs the old-fashioned way. This was no Kodak Film Tank such as Barry Armstrong used.

A swift perusal of the pictures confirmed my fears that they contained more revolting pornographic exposures of a woman in various positions of partial or full nudity. I was about to expostulate on such filth, when Holmes hissed and grabbed me by the arm to warn me to be silent. He motioned me back onto the landing and I followed him as he opened the third door.

We entered another lounge which was half-lit by an old-fashioned gas lamp on a mantelpiece. A surge of stifling heat hit us like a tidal wave. The curtains on the window were pulled across, giving the room an eerie, theatrical atmosphere. There was another bed in a corner, a chesterfield and several easy chairs. Mozart's Clarinet Concerto played softly in the background, presumably from a wax gramophone record.

'Welcome, Sherlock,' came a disembodied wheeze from the sofa. 'You *have* taken your time. So you got my message?'

'Indeed. Although I imagined it might have come from ... someone else.'

'Oh, do not worry,' came another gasp. 'The glorious Professor really did die at the Reichenbach Falls. Whereas I got to spend a mere three decades of my life in jail, thanks to your meddling interference! And now at last the time has come to pay the price. What was it you said to me, all those years ago? *Journeys end in lovers' meetings*, wasn't it? Well, Holmes. Someone's journey has certainly come to an end now.'

The mirthless voice gave way to an imposing figure that rose from the chesterfield. Even without his hoary moustache, and given the passage of time, I recognised his swarthy features and that high bald forehead. Moran! Colonel Sebastian Moran! Moriarty's henchman! Once the second most dangerous man in London! Sebastian's grandfather, who was pointing a rifle at my friend. I raised the Webley in earnest.

'Careful, Watson,' warned Holmes. 'Pocket your revolver for the time being. I am sure we would both like to hear the true story of how one of Queen Victoria's keenest soldiers and the best heavy game shikari in the Eastern Empire has sunk so low as to become involved in the filthy business of pornography, to the extent of even using his own children as bait for willing customers. And possibly killing some of them in the process. Or even worse, if one considers the corpse of your unfortunate disabled daughter next door. Speak up, Moran. We are listening.'

'Oh, you *have* got the wrong end of the stick entirely, Sherlock. It is not as bad as you may think,' panted the old man. He paused, to ingest something from an aerosol inhaler. Ephedrine, I guessed. He was obviously suffering from chronic asthma.

'First of all,' he continued. 'Let me congratulate you on finally discovering the photograph I had subtly placed in the music satchel. You did not observe my action, did you, doctor, outside Armstrong's leather goods shop that cold day last January?'

'Certainly not,' I replied. My hand remained on the comforting weight of the revolver in my pocket. If he showed any sign of firing at Holmes, I would shoot him first through the lining.

'I was wearing my trilby and muffler, as I do on the rare occasions when I venture out nowadays. One cannot be too careful. I knew you were buying it for your music-loving friend's birthday, and I hoped the photo would intrigue the world's first consulting detective, and bring him within my paltry dominion. Nevertheless, I must confess it *was* a spur of the moment thing, and I am absolutely delighted that my little plan has worked. Even with a seven month delay.'

'Did you take that filthy picture of your own poor daughter?' I demanded.

'No,' replied Moran. 'I did not. Nor did I take any of those other photographs next door. They are not my style. Why don't we all sit down, like civilised people, while I explain everything to you both? You take those two seats, and please keep your hands where I can see them. That's better, doctor.'

Moran sank back onto the chesterfield with an audible sigh. It occurred to me he must be well into his eighties by now. That could be an advantage to us, if there was to be any shooting.

'You may not know that my real name is Sebastian Bosanquet,' he continued. 'I changed it to Moran when I entered Her Majesty's Service, as I felt that my Huguenot ancestry might cause me problems, both in my regiment and with my family. You may also be unaware that I was the proud father of eight daughters before you pair of bumbling amateurs had me incarcerated for killing that pipsqueak loser Adair.'

'And for attempting to shoot Holmes!' I burst out indignantly.

'Yes, yes. The Von Herder air-gun trick worked once, didn't it? But not twice. Ah, well. Third time lucky, eh? We shall see. At least you are not a dummy now, Sherlock. And this is not an air-gun. In fact it is a single trigger double-barrelled shotgun, capable of blasting both of you to kingdom come within a second. I adapted it myself. To continue. Because of the damage to the family's reputation during my time in prison, my socially conscious wife divorced me, and seven of my daughters renounced their father, refusing to have anything further to do with him. Even my grandchildren are forbidden to visit me, at her instigation. The only child who cared about me, and who visited me in prison regularly, before coming to live with me after I got out, was the youngest, my poor little Nicole, whose damaged body lies in the next room, awaiting instructions from my wife concerning her burial.'

I snorted in derision.

'I suppose there is also a good reason as to why she is not clothed?'

'Is she naked? I have not been able to look. She only died a few days ago, from the brain disease her birth had created. My wife arranged for the preparation of the body, and I have not entered the room since. She is to be buried next week. You see, gentlemen, my youngest daughter, sweet Nicole, was not born with just a physical disability. Her birth was an horrendous affair, taking many days, the result of which was a certain degree of brain damage when she finally arrived. Nicole was a simple soul, whose great joys in her childlike life were music and later on, photography. A mental age of ten or twelve at the best, we were told by the physician. Perhaps that is why she did not form any of the prejudice against me that was so prevalent in her mother and sisters. She was always my favourite child. I might even say our bond went beyond what would be considered normal between a father and daughter.'

'I can imagine,' I blurted out, only to find Holmes' cautionary hand yet again upon my arm. My friend's nostrils flared wildly and there was a look of fierce concentration on his face, sure signs that he was becoming more interested in Moran's story. If I did not know any better, I might even suggest that he was actually getting ... excited.

'She would practice for hours on the viola I bought her for her tenth birthday. There was little talent, of course, but she was not aware of that. I suppose music was just a sound to her, one that she enjoyed. Then, after I came out of prison, we would spend many an evening here together, listening to Mozart on my gramophone. She called him Upstart, which she found very funny. Mollie, my housekeeper, looked after her for me. They share ... shared another room.'

'So who took that damned photograph of her in a semi-naked state, then?' I cried.

Moran began a coughing fit that lasted for at least a minute. It was another full minute before he had recovered sufficiently to answer my question. During that time, I managed to slip my hand gently around my gun.

'Why, she took it herself, of course. As she took all of the other pictures in the next room. In the privacy of the back garden. She loved to dress up and experiment with different poses. Some of them might be considered pornographic by the standards of modern society, but that was just her innocence, really. Gentlemen, Nicole was not aware her sexual organs should be considered in any way differently from either her face, legs or hands. Despite being in her forties, she would never have experienced what others call *adult* love. And apart from your good selves, and Mollie, nobody else has, and ever will, see those self-portraits.'

'Then why did she look as though she was pleading with the photographer, in the one you slipped into the music satchel?' queried Holmes. 'And exactly how could she have taken them herself? It is physically impossible!'

'You disappoint me, Sherlock,' panted Moran. 'I always imagined you would keep up to date on all subjects of interest to the scientific mind. People have been taking pictures of themselves since the first daguerreotype. In fact I purchased a spring-powered, pneumatic delay Kodak self-timing camera for Nicole soon after I had finished with His Majesty's pleasure. If my darling daughter looks anxious in that photo, it is because she is concerned it will not develop properly. There is no other reason.'

'It is true that I cannot admit to a passion for the recording of the self, in any form,' muttered Holmes. He sounded more disappointed at being so wrong in his deduction about the look on Nicole's face and her musical prowess, than angry at having led us both into the simple trap laid by Colonel Sebastian Moran, who was now raising his rifle and pointing it at my friend.

'That is quite enough exposition,' he gasped. 'Time for your journey's end, Mister Sherlock Bloody Holmes.'

That was when I squeezed the trigger within my pocket. Through the lining of my jacket.

It was well after midnight by the time we arrived safely back at Baker Street, after the usual explanations with Jasper Lestrade and Scotland Yard. A thoughtful Lily Hudson had laid out an excellent cold plate for us – duck, turkey, potato salad and beetroot – with a bottle of her best Claret to wash it down. We tucked in gratefully, and only talked about the case once we had settled ourselves in our chairs and lit our final pipes of the day.

'So you were completely wrong about the lady in the pornographic photograph needing your help, Holmes. The whole business was just some kind of spontaneous trap. Although I have no idea how you seem to have known that the picture was a message to you.'

'Yes. Perhaps I am still too haunted by the ghost of Professor Moriarty, and see his hand in too many places,' replied my colleague, drawing deeply on his clay pipe. 'I admit this case has developed in a way I did not expect. Had we found that photograph earlier in the year, when Nicole Bosanquet was still alive, and followed it up then, the result might have been entirely different.'

'What do you mean?' I demanded. 'I don't understand. I killed that villain Moran with my first shot, before he could get one off at us.'

Holmes grimaced at the memory. 'Oh, Watson. My dear chap. Don't you understand? You did exactly what he *wanted* you to do. I checked his shotgun after Lestrade arrived. There were no cartridges in it.'

'What?' I ejaculated. 'Empty? Then why ...?'

'I can only guess that the death of his beloved daughter caused him to change his plans to do away with us if we *did* manage to turn up. While he was speaking, I sensed that he wanted a different outcome. One where we killed *him,* rather than him killing us.'

'But why bother with all that? Why not just commit suicide?'

Holmes sucked in a lungful of tobacco smoke before exhaling it slowly. 'Because the old hunter had an opportunity to involve us in his murder, and hoped we would be prosecuted for same, and either be hung, or spend the rest of our lives in Pentonville Jail. It was a final trap. He did not know that we have a close relationship with a certain Scotland Yard Detective Inspector, who will ensure you are not arraigned for the killing of the old lag. Self defence, etcetera, etcetera.'

'Oh, that is such a relief,' I muttered wearily.

'He was probably dying anyway,' continued my friend, who was clearly enjoying himself a little at my expense. 'I am sure you also checked his handkerchief afterwards. The blood suggests tuberculosis.'

I decided to return his serve with interest.

'And he had asthma. You know, Holmes, this has definitely not been one of your best cases. Barry Armstrong had nothing to do with it, contrary to your intuition. Also Nicole Bosanquet was neither kidnapped, Jewish, a professional musician, a friend of Jesenia Marple, a drug-addict or South American. Although there is a possibility she may have smoked cigarettes and used reading glasses.'

'Indeed. You are correct,' he countered immediately. 'Her dilated pupils were probably connected to her birth defect. But although she was middle-aged, she had no children, the wedding ring was obviously wishful thinking on her part, as were the necklace and the fancy clothes. She was youthful-looking in herself and not a prostitute. Neither was she in love with the cameraman or just plain cold. In fact she was merely worried about her damn camera working properly.'

'Oh, well. I give up,' I yawned. 'Game, set and match. Do you know, this might be our last case together. I must start writing it up tomorrow.'

'Last case?' muttered Holmes, puzzled. Then it dawned on him. 'My dear chap, I had forgotten entirely about your damned illness. Yet again. Do forgive me.'

'Oh, never mind,' I grunted. 'Have you got another of those tablets of yours? It may help me to sleep tonight.'

It appeared that some things would never change. After all, this was the same friend who had disappeared from my life for a painful hiatus of three years, casually leaving me to mourn his passing in grief-stricken loneliness, for reasons which have never been fully acceptable to his so-called Boswell.

14. Sherlock Holmes And The Camden Counterfeiter.

'I perceive that you have succeeded in committing yet another silent bank robbery, Watson,' chuckled Sherlock Holmes, flicking his newspaper over a page. 'The Capital and Counties this time. With a Webley, too! And quite a significant haul. A thousand pounds! You must be a rich man. Can you lend me a tenner or two?'

'Very funny, Holmes.'

I was in no mood for my friend's warped sense of humour, having already perused the same Times article of Monday, July 15th, 1929, which illustrated its scandalous content with an apparent photograph of me, albeit when I seemed younger, smiling away and in better health. I still had my whiskers and almost a full head of hair. As far as I was concerned, this dopplegänger was a vile criminal, who saw nothing wrong in depriving innocent people of their life savings, and on another occasion, shooting and critically injuring a bank clerk. He had the cheek to leave a snapshot of yours truly behind each time. Anyway, the fact that he looked like me was irrelevant to someone who was dying of cancer and had only a number of months to live. Why should I care a whit?

The reality of my passing was something I had grown well used to over the last two years. Knowing that my redeemer liveth, I was now looking forward to being with my beloved wives, Mary and Beatrice once again in the hereafter, that splendid valley where all paths meet.

'At least you have an alibi,' continued Holmes. 'Stuck in that bed over there, it is extremely unlikely you could have flown out the window like a magpie and over to Camden Town to pull off this job.'

'True,' I countered. 'Also your reputation as my associate will manage to remain intact.'

Lily Hudson, our landlady, and her husband Jasper Lestrade had moved me from my room upstairs to the corner of the sitting room in 221B Baker Street. So they could keep an eye on me, they claimed. As Holmes had become less interested in chemistry, his equipment was swapped for my bed on the second floor. I had lost so much weight over the preceding six months that I was too weak to get about on my own very much. Unfortunately, this meant that the disgusting adventure of the Portobello Pornographer almost a year earlier was to become my last case as an active assistant to the world's first consulting detective.

The tables had been turned, and instead of Holmes injecting himself with morphine, it was myself whom he treated with the painkiller. Nowadays the throbs from my ancient Maiwand wounds had faded into insignificance in comparison to the discomfort eminating from my cancerous colon and liver. When not suffering too much, my pastimes included the documentation of his remaining untold adventures, including this highly personal one, and playing with the latest addition to the household, who had become, at twenty-one months, a fully-fledged toddler.

'Oh, dear God. Here he comes again,' muttered Holmes, hiding behind the newspaper.

Lily and Jasper's son, Sherlock George, had taken to climbing up the seventeen stairs of 221B in order to play with his ailing godfather. It cheered me up no end to have him around for a short while during each day, but his presence merely irritated my friend.

'Good morning, old chap,' I cried from my bed. 'Oh, do look, Holmes. The delightful fellow is standing up already. And he's trying to walk over to me ... be careful, Junior ... oops a daisy!'

But the plucky little shaver took his fall gracefully, stood up again and continued unsteadily on his path towards me. Then he propped himself against the bed and held out his hands as usual, so that I could lift him up beside me. It was an act I was capable of now, but for how much longer?

'Ga-ga, ga-ga!' he cried. 'Goo-goo, doo-doo, poo-poo?'

'This is all too much excitement for me,' exclaimed Holmes. He snapped his newspaper onto the cane sofa, stretched his arms out wide, rose to his feet, cracked his dottles pipe-bowl against the hearth, grabbed his hat and cape and headed for the door.

'I am going out for the day. I shall inform Lily that she must administer your drugs when necessary.'

'But why don't you stay for a while? You could play with your namesake?' I cried. 'He would just love that.'

In fact, Sherlock Junior was terrified of the great detective, and would cuddle up beside me in bed fearfully whenever Holmes opened his mouth. As he did now.

But the sleuth was gone, still fit enough at seventy-five to take the stairs two at a time, as though he could not wait to escape his ailing partner in crime and a certain happy little lad who shared his name.

'So. What shall we read today, my beamish boy? Callooh! Callay!' I chortled. 'Let us see.'

I leaned across the bedside table and grabbed a handful of children's books.

'What about Winnie-The-Pooh?'

'Tiggah. Tiggah.'

We had shared the adventures of the teddy bear and his friends Christopher Robin, Tigger and Eeyore in the Hundred Acre Wood several times already. I wanted to familiarise young Sherlock with the best of children's literature, so he would continue to enjoy stories after I was gone, and read for himself as he was growing up. It was my private hope that he would not develop into an alienated, sociopathic, heartless, inhuman, drug-addicted, single-minded, unemotional machine like his namesake.

'Here is Edward Bear, coming down the stairs now, bump bump bump, on the back of his head, behind Christopher Robin ...'

Lily clumped her way upstairs to collect my godson after an hour, which was about the limit of my energy. I spent the rest of the morning dozing on and off, until she returned with some spinach soup for my lunch. Food had always been a serious pleasure to me, but now that I was confined to quarters, so to speak, and forbidden even the occasional brandy, it had assumed a vitally significant importance in each day's boring routine. Even spinach soup.

My illness and the presence of young Sherlock's joyful innocence had reminded me of my own childhood, a subject I considered lost for many years. They say the mind plays games with our memories as we age. This may well explain my increasing recollection of that idyllic boyhood as I lay in bed, while at the same time not being able to remember what I had eaten for breakfast the previous day.

My elder brother Henry and I were born in the Hampshire town of Winchester. Being a civil servant of a certain rank, our father Jack was quite well off, so we never went without, and may even have been spoiled, especially by our darling Scottish mother. Unfortunately Ella Watson passed away when I was only six, and subsequently my father emigrated to Australia with his two boys in tow. He prospered in the burgeoning Melbourne suburb of St Kilda, where our conventional middle-class family life continued. We had an Irish nanny there, whom we both grew to love. Eventually my father remarried.

There were the customary Bible Classes on Sunday afternoons, combined with Morning and Evening Prayers in the local Anglican Church. We did all the usual dangerous things that young boys should do – hiking, camping, climbing trees, sword-fighting, fishing, swimming, rugby in the winter, cricket in the summer. I was quite upset when father decided to return to England in 1865 and send us both as day boarders to Wellington College in Hampshire. But I adjusted swiftly and grew to thrive on the discipline of the English public school system. Whereas Henry did not.

My brother was a complete layabout, even as a child. Although he enjoyed sports at school, and made the first eleven rugby squad, the word *study* was a random selection of five letters in the English alphabet to him. Consequently, he flunked his final exams and our father had to find him a position in a friend's firm as a trainee salesman of typewriter ribbons.

It has always bothered me that our father seemed to favour my brother over me. While I was working my way through college and the army, followed by the experience of a horrifying war or two, he was gallivanting around the pubs of London and cavorting with loose women. To cut a long story short, Henry threw away his chances, lived for some time in poverty, with occasional short intervals of prosperity and finally, taking to drink, died at the age of thirty-seven. Most of his sad story had been deduced by Holmes many years earlier, from an old fifty-guinea watch I showed him.

After school, I studied medicine at St Bartholomew's, and was subsequently trained at the military hospital in Netley as an assistant surgeon in the British Army. From there I joined the 5th Northumberland Fusiliers in India, before being transferred to the 66th (Berkshire) Regiment of Foot in the second Anglo-Afghan war. This was followed by those infamous Maiwand wounds, rescue by my orderly Murray, enteric fever at a Peshawar hospital and a full medical discharge with pension, all career regressions I would dearly love to forget.

One thing had always puzzled me as a lad. On our return to England, his second wife having also passed away in Australia, our father used to drink a good deal at the weekends. When he was in his cups, he might forget or confuse the names of his two sons. He would cuff me heartily around the ear and call me Henry or James, while Henry became John or James. Or we could both be Jamsie or Jamie. Each of our middle names was Hamish, and it *is* the Scottish form of James, but this habit of his had raised question marks in my mind over recent years, having so much time on my hands.

I resolved to ask Holmes for advice about these lingering shadows from my childhood when he returned from his day's outing.

My friend entered just as Lily was setting the table for dinner, around six-thirty. He went directly into his room without a word.

'Cain yer si' dawn a' taible, Watsey?' she enquired.

'Yes, of course,' I grunted, stepping out of bed and donning my dressing-gown. 'What's for dinner anyway?'

'Chick'n an' brocchli baike, wiv toinips.'

'Wonderful.' Turnips. I had a sudden memory of my mother telling me to be a good boy and eat up my 'bottled sunshine'. A healthy diet. What I wouldn't have given for a hefty sirloin steak, with fried onions and creamed potatoes, washed down by a decent claret. Ah, well.

'Holmes!' I called. 'Are you joining us?'

'In a moment.'

'What have you been up to?' I asked, when he finally appeared at the table, clad in his mousy dressing-gown and smoking a Chesterfield.

'It was your comment about my reputation that inspired me,' he replied, enigmatically.

'Inspired you to do what, exactly?'

'To spend the day with my old college chum Algernon Carpenter at the General Register Office in Somerset House. I wondered if this lookalike criminal might be related to you in some way.'

'And is he?'

Holmes mashed his cigarette on a saucer and picked up his knife and fork.

'We will discuss the subject after dinner. It might be better if you processed my news upon a full stomach.'

'Well?' I enquired, when we had both finished our meal, and were sitting comfortably in front of a crackling fire, our pipes ablaze and creating a swirling fug of smoke around the room.

Holmes shifted awkwardly in his chair.

'What can you remember about your childhood?' he asked. 'How far back can you go?'

'Oh, let me think. Probably to when I was about three, and my father made me this wonderful box tricycle. It was painted jet black, and I could pedal it around our garden at what I considered to be the speed of a galloping racehorse. Before that is just a hazy cloud of happiness. I remember my mother spoiling my brother Henry and I quite a lot. After she died, life became more ... difficult. But our father loved us and everything was still perfectly normal, considering such a profound loss at a young age. Why do you ask?'

'John. I want you to prepare yourself for a shock. Are you ready for that?'

I leaned forward and looked at Holmes to ensure he was being serious. He so rarely called me by my Christian name that I was quite alarmed. And his fingers were bridged against his lips, which usually meant a degree of complexity in his thinking.

'Of course I am. What are you saying? Come on, man! Don't keep me in suspense, for God's sake!'

'All right. First of all, can you confirm that you were born on August 7th, 1852?'

'You are perfectly aware that is my date of birth, Holmes.'

'Yes, I suppose I am. You know, old fellow. None of us can control the circumstances of our birth.'

'Will you stop beating about the bush and explain yourself!' I exclaimed angrily.

'O, very well,' he sighed. 'Here goes. Your father was not your real father.'

'What in blazes!' I was close to flinging myself at the man, despite my weakened state.

'Calm down and I will explain. Sit back there. That's it. Old Algernon was of considerable assistance to me in my quest, as he had spent the last two years in charge of a team whose remit was the collation of all births, marriages and deaths within the United Kingdom into one central file in Somerset House. Records already existed, of course, but the job of his team was to travel around the country, examining the church registers of every village and town in the land, with a view to updating those files. A procedure has now been set in place whereby all future births, marriages and deaths must be communicated to Somerset House within one month, on penalty of a hefty fine. Regardless of religion.'

'And?' I queried impatiently.

'And we had no trouble finding the record for the birth of your brother Henry, on September 18th, 1850, to your parents. But we could find *no* record of the birth of a John Hamish to an Ella and Jack Watson, in St Mary's Church at Teddington, the town you grew up in, on August 7th, 1852. None.'

'None?' I ehoed weakly.

'However, there *is* a record of the birth of a John Hamish Sacker to an Ella Watson and Ormond Sacker for the same day, in that same place. A couple who were marked as being unmarried. But there is no record of any formal adoption, of course.'

'Ormond Sacker?' I squawked. 'John Sacker? There must be some mistake, that's all. These records are obviously not reliable.' Ormond Sacker indeed! Who did Holmes think he was kidding?

'There's more,' said Holmes.

'There's more?' More than being told my father was not my birth father? That I was, in fact, illegitimate? Born out of wedlock? A bastard?

'Yes. On the same day, several minutes later, one Jamie Sacker was born to your mother. You have a twin, Watson, who was obviously not raised within your family. That might go some way to explaining the dopplegänger affect of our bank robber, don't you agree? He could be the offspring of your sibling, who is hell bent upon revenge for what he perceives as his family's blighted treatment.'

Jamie. Jamsie. I could almost feel my father's drunken clout around my ear. My brain raced. He must have known about this other baby. And that he was not my real father. His wife's lover, Ormond Sacker was the real father of us both. There was probably an arrangement to split the twins up. Now those shadows were beginning to clear. This would explain my father's preference for Henry over me. But could my twin really be related to the Camden bank robber? A damned criminal?'

'Is there eh, any ... record of what happened to this ... Jamie person and his f...f...father?' I stammered.

'Eh ... *her* father. Your fraternal twin was female, Watson. You were not identical. The answer is no. I spent a good deal of time checking the births, marriages and deaths for the next forty years, and the name Sacker is never mentioned again. They may have changed their name or emigrated, of course. You were probably called Watson to avoid complications. I know this is difficult for you, but at least your mother and father did choose you ahead of Jamie.'

But why? Surely my mother would have wanted a girl after having Henry? None of this made any sense.

Watson, Sacker. Sacker, Watson. A female twin. Good Lord! How dearly I would have loved a sister!

'Is there anything else you have not told me?' I asked.

Holmes took small rapid puffs from his glowing pipe and stared fixedly into the fire.

'No. Wait. Eh, Ormond Sacker was a clergyman. That's it. One of your lot. Where, it did not say.'

My birth father was an Anglican preacher. Great Scott! Suddenly I felt most dreadfully tired. And bloody angry. I did not want to hear any more.

'I shall go to bed now,' I muttered. 'This bastard can't take all this in at the moment. It might have been better if you had waited until the morning to tell me. Or perhaps you could have chosen not to torment me at all with this damned information when I have only a few months to live. I always knew you to be an unfeeling fellow, but you have outdone yourself in callousness this time, Holmes.'

'There is a very good reason, old chap,' he replied swiftly. 'That bank clerk has died. So your dopplegänger, relation or not, is now a murderer as well as a thief. I need your help in capturing him. I cannot do it alone. Other people's lives may be at stake. And you are not a bastard, in the true sense of the word. Your mother and adoptive father would have signed forms for you, but no records of adoptions were kept until recently.'

Other people's lives! What about *mine*! A life lived as a lie! And how could he be sure that *any* documents were signed at the time?

'The crime. It's always about the crime with you, isn't it? What about the *people*? Well, I really don't know. Perhaps I shall think about it overnight.'

I heaved a sigh, doffed my dressing-gown and climbed back into bed, before turning my face abruptly to the wall. 'Just put the light out when you go to your room, would you, please, Holmes?'

'Certainly. I shall do that now. Don't forget to take your painkiller. Good night, old fellow.'

I passed a horribly restless night, tossing and turning and dreaming that I was already in my grave, yet still alive, like Holmes and I had been in the case of the Acton Body-Snatchers. Instead of the great detective, this time it was my unknown doppelgänger who entered the nightmare and lay beside me in my coffin, whispering into my ear the words, '*Just wait until you see my next trick, Johnnie boy. It will be miraculous*'. That woke me up immediately and I lay on my side, heart pounding, terrified. For a second, I did not know where I was. Or where that unfamiliar smell was coming from. And what was the faint whistling sound?

When I recovered, still groggy from lack of sleep, and with a stiff neck, I could swear I heard the door to our sitting room closing softly. Assuming it was Holmes off on some nocturnal jaunt, and not caring one way or the other what he got up to any more, I took another sleeping draught, closed my eyes and tried not to think about the stunning news Holmes had provided the previous evening. A father and sister I had never known, a mother who chose me over that sister and a life that had been lived in ignorance of the fact? Son of a clergyman? Relatives who might be crooks? And only a few months left to think about it all? How could anybody sleep with such news?

Finally I managed to re-enter a drugged slumberland and was only woken in the early morning by a shout from Holmes as he opened his door into the sitting room, heading for the bathroom.

'What in blazes?' he cried. 'Do wake up, Watson, and peruse the wall. It would seem we have had a visitor during the night. Either that, or you have taken to pointillism during your sleep.'

I sat up abruptly and stared at the wall above my bed. There, painted in bright red dots below some scientific charts, were four letters: DIEB, followed by a dot. They looked like the VR Holmes had outlined with bullets in a fit of boredom many years earlier, in homage to Her Majesty, Queen Victoria.

'Good God, Holmes. Dieb! What can it mean?'

'I believe someone is calling you names, Watson. *Dieb* is the German word for *thief.*'

Only then did last night's revelations come flooding back, followed by the intruder into my nasty dream. Could it be ... ?

I swiftly explained the message our visitor had so obviously whispered into my ear.

'*Miraculous.* Hmmm. And still you did not wake up?'

'I did. I heard the door closing and assumed it was you leaving the room.'

'Well. I suppose we should be thankful that you were not harmed in any way. Your blood might well have been used for the message instead of paint.'

Holmes sounded almost disappointed, as though any damage to my good self might have provided him with more clues to solve the case.

'What is wrong with your neck, Watson?'

'Oh, just a little stiff.'

'Right. Let us see what this message tells us,' he mused.

'Never mind that, Holmes,' I said, thoroughly annoyed, and not a little frightened. 'How did the damn fellow get into our sitting room in the middle of the night? Don't you feel threatened? He could have entered your room and stuck a knife in your throat!'

'Why don't you go down to Lily and ask her that very question, Watson?' he replied calmly. 'Meanwhile I intend to examine this room thoroughly. It is not often we have an actual crime – breaking and entering – occurring within the very confines of 221B Baker Street. The most obvious clue is that our visitor has read some of your overblown renditions of past cases, specifically the dramatically titled *Study In Scarlet*. I think we can assume he is *not* of German extraction.'

That magnifying glass had materialised again, like a rabbit out of a pocket.

An hour later I climbed back up the stairs, somewhat down at heart, and worrying what Holmes might say about my innocent young godchild, who had grabbed the keys off a shelf in the kitchen, and clearly dropped them somewhere outside on the road. So Lily had surmised, after she had seen him playing with them and subsequently had to use her husband's set. I asked her to change the locks on the front door immediately.

I found the great detective down on all fours, in full hound dog mode, sniffing around the base of my bed.

'Young Sherlock must have thrown the keys out of the pram, Holmes. That is Lily's belief, anyway.'

'Then our house is being watched and she is being followed,' he grunted. 'Your double would hardly have found them by accident. The locks will have to be altered, of course.'

'Yes. That will happen today. I am going to have a bath. Have you discovered anything yet?'

'Not much yet, Watson. Apart from many confusing outlines of that same blasted child's feet. But whatever I find can wait until after you have cleansed your body.'

'Interestingly, old chap, the words on the wall were not made with paint after all,' said Holmes, once I had returned to the sitting room and the sofa in front of Lily's early morning fire. 'Unless I am very much mistaken, the appalling odour suggests that nitrocellulose was used.'

'And what is that when it is at home in Baker Street?' I enquired, filling my briar with Arcadia ship's tobacco.

'Car paint and film celluloid is made with it, and the liquid polish some women see fit to smear upon their fingernails. We might have to revisit the theory that your deadly doppelgänger is your nephew, and think of him as a possible *her*. Your *niece*. Did the voice sound like that of a female?'

'I couldn't tell. I thought I was dreaming, remember?'

'Accent?'

'None that I could detect. So what else have you established?'

'Nothing. She left no traces on the floor, bed, wall, stairs or doors. But this absence of evidence is evidence in itself. It confirms in my mind the fact that she is a professional burglar, as well as a competent actress and bank robber. We know from the newspaper reports that she disguises herself to look like you, so we have no way of knowing her real appearance.'

'Or if she is, in fact, related to me at all,' I pointed out.

'True. The only clues we have are the word DIEB and her threat of a miraculous event. I suppose I should warn Lestrade about that. Hark! Speak of the devil. I believe this might be him now.'

I could hear nothing, but as that faculty had deteriorated over the years, I was not altogether surprised when Jasper Lestrade knocked gently on the door before entering, twisting the rim of his bowler hat around his hands, over-respectful to the great detective as per usual.

'Gentlemen. A good morning to you both. I do hope you are feeling better today, Dr. Watson?'

I wasn't, but manners maketh the man. So my adoptive father had repeatedly told me anyway.

'Yes, thank you, Jasper. Any sign of breakfast?'

'It's on its way. Eh, there has been another incident involving the Camden robber overnight.'

'Overnight?' Holmes and I chorused in harmony.

'Indeed. Are you both familiar with the new Carerras tobacco factory in Mornington Crescent? The Arcadia Works? Opened last year?'

'I am,' replied Holmes. 'But the good doctor has not seen it yet, due to his illness.'

'That is correct,' I concurred. 'I believe it is of considerable architectural interest, with an art deco Egyptian colonnade and cat motifs on the facade. And they manufacture many new brands of cigars and cigarettes. I have sampled a few boxes Holmes purchased for me.'

'Yes. Eh, pardon me, but before I go any further I need to confirm you were both here last night, and did not venture out.' Lestrade's ferret features were flushed with embarrassment.

'Of course. Now tell us more about this incident,' demanded Holmes.

'Well. There were two enormous bronze black cats at the entrance. Guarding it, like.'

'And each representing the Egyptian God *Bastet*, daughter of *Ra, the sun god,*' commented Holmes patiently. 'It is also known as The Black Cat factory. You used the word *were?*'

'They were not so much stolen, as *moved*. During the night.'

'To where?' Holmes and I, in unison again.

'That's the thing, see. They are now perched outside this house, complete with plinths. Number 221B. On the steps.'

'What in blazes?' I cried.

'And there is a photograph of you, Doctor Watson, slipped under one of them, just as in the bank robberies. Here it is.'

'Good grief.' I could think of nothing else to say, as I stared yet again at that old familiar head, years before it had become bald and grey and withered. With a shock I realised the grainy newspaper picture had obscured the most important factor in this case.

'Holmes?'

'Yes, Watson?'

'I'm afraid your theory of a doppelgänger may not be so accurate after all.'

'Why?'

'Because this is an *actual* photograph of me, taken about twenty years ago, when my practice in Paddington was going well, and my second wife Beatrice and I had just been married. Ah, yes! I remember now! It was taken at our wedding, and appeared in the Times.'

'But one of the clerks in the Capital and Counties confirmed that the robber was identical to the person in the photograph,' insisted Lestrade.

'So it changes very little,' remarked Holmes. 'You are still being framed for these crimes, Watson. That was clear to me from the start.'

At this stage the great detective brought Lestrade up to date about our intruder, the word on the wall, the threat about a miracle, and his theory that a woman may be at the bottom of the crimes. Thank heavens he mentioned nothing about my dubious ancestry.

'Perhaps the Times newspaper would have a record of anyone who asked for a copy of that photo?' I suggested.

'Good point, doctor. We shall certainly check it out,' replied Lestrade.

'Were there no security guards outside the factory?' I asked.

'Yes, of course,' replied Lestrade. 'But he was on his rounds to the rear of the building. It takes him about ten minutes every hour.'

'Four minutes to remove the cats, followed by six minutes to get them into the van or lorry. So they knew his routine. I'd like to see our two felines, in the bronze, so to speak,' said Holmes. 'Coming, Doctor? I'll help you down the stairs.'

'Thank you, Holmes,' I replied gruffly. 'I can still make my own way with the cane.'

'At least the fog has lifted,' muttered Lestrade. 'I have to warn you both that Lily is beside herself with rage at this stunt. There is quite a crowd outside, including several reporters.'

'In that case, I am definitely making an appearance. It is about time these hacks saw the real Dr. Watson as he is today,' I grimaced. 'How could a poor old character like me rob a bank, I ask you?'

'Oi wan' 'em payer o' tommies offen moi staips afore ternoight. 'em's baid luk, so 'ey is!'

Lily's shrill voice followed us out the front door onto the street, where Lestrade was forced to move a small crowd back to make way for our examination of two enormous statues of black cats. I knew nothing about ancient Egyptian gods, but even I could tell that they were over eight feet tall, and well beyond the scope of one person to move. Especially a member of the fair sex.

Holmes pushed hard against one of them, to no effect. Then the glass appeared again, and he spent several minutes examining the pair and the plinths upon which they rested majestically, their yellow eyes staring blankly above the heads of the fascinated crowd.

'Miaow, miaow,' came from some wit at the back.

'What are their names, eh? Holmes and Watson?' This fatuous comment was uttered by a scruffy, well-known lackey from the Herald, a newspaper that made the Daily Mail read like the King James Version of the Bible.

'That's put the cats among the pigeon,' shouted another wag.

'It's enough to make two cats laugh.'

Holmes ignored the crowd entirely.

'How could they have been moved all the way over here?' I asked Lestrade.

'That is what we will have to find out,' he replied. 'Hopefully Mr Holmes ...?'

'At least two strong people, with some sort of transportation,' replied the man himself, standing up. 'Each of whom was above average height, wearing brown leather gloves and grey trousers. Can we get rid of this mob, Lestrade? I wish to examine the street.'

Jasper produced his Scotland Yard badge of office and called out: 'All right, that's enough. Just move along now. Go to your homes. Else you will be had up for disturbing the peace.'

Most of the crowd gradually dispersed, leaving a few wide-eyed stragglers on the far side of the road.

Holmes sank onto his knees and stretched his body along the gutter, glass to eye, fingers spread over the ground, muttering to himself about dust and shoes and tyres.

'But why go to all this trouble? That's what I would like to know,' I wondered aloud.

'Presumably this is the miraculous trick of your intruder,' Lestrade said. 'He or she must be one of the two clowns who are responsible. Or it may be a warning of some kind. As Lily says, black cats do mean bad luck.'

Holmes sprang back up onto his feet and dusted down his trousers.

'Damnation! Too many idle neer-do-wells hanging around to find out anything useful from the street itself. Lestrade, you can arrange for the two statues to be taken back to their rightful abode. Before that, I would like to see the entrance to the Carerras factory over in Mornington Crescent and speak to the nightwatchman. We can take the Underground. Watson, you do not need to come with me. I shall report back to you later on.'

Despite a faint regret that I would not be joining Holmes on his investigation, I must admit I was only too happy to avoid the dreaded twopenny tube and get back to the warmth and comfort of our sitting room, where I could anticipate my regular daily visit from Sherlock Junior.

'These are for you, old friend.'

Holmes returned to our room in the early evening, waking me up from a fireside doze by placing a packet of Black Cat cigarettes gently upon my lap.

'Get back, you bloody towelhead! Take that! What the blazes? Oh, thank you, Holmes. Most thoughtful. Hah! Black Cat, eh? Are they gone? Have you made any progress?'

'The feline pair are now back in their rightful place. And yes, indeed. I have made a small progress,' he replied, grabbing his persian slipper and flinging himself onto the cane chair.

'Fortunately Mornington Crescent had not been entirely corrupted by a gawping crowd, so I was able to identify the type of lorry used by the number of wheels and density of tyre tracks outside the factory both before and after the cats were loaded. Lestrade then quickly established that a six-wheel covered Super Sentinel steam wagon had been reported stolen overnight from a builder's garage in Camden High Street.'

Holmes paused to set fire to his cherrywood with a blazing Vesta flame.

'But how on earth could such a noisy vehicle be driven over here during the night without anyone noticing?' I demanded.

'Indeed. And back to Hampstead Heath, where it was discovered late this afternoon, upside down in a ditch,' he replied. 'I shall take a look at it tomorrow. It would have been noticed, I imagine, but such nocturnal journeys are not that unusual these days, even with two big cats aboard.'

'Twin cats,' I muttered.

'Indeed. Twins. An image that ties in rather too neatly with your newfound family history and the recent burglaries. Is there really nothing else you can remember from your childhood that could be of assistance? For instance, when your mother died, did you attend her funeral?'

'No. Both Henry and I wanted to, but our father would not permit it. We remained at home with our maid, Gladys.'

'And would you have a photograph of your mother?'

'No. That is something I have always regretted. But why on earth do you need one? What else did you discover?'

Holmes waved his pipe casually in the direction of the fire.

'Oh, just a thought,' he muttered. 'Our friends used a jimmy bar to dislodge the cats from their plinths, which would not have been easy, especially as it had to be done swiftly. Judging by the footprints near the tracks, there were three people involved, one of whom may have been a woman or a child. The nightwatchman actually heard the steam wagon taking off in our direction, but did not realise what they were up to until he reached the front entrance.'

'That must have given him a bit of a fright!' I joked.

'He is an ex-policeman himself, so he was quick to blow his whistle. But the wagon was well gone by the time anyone responded.'

———————————

Watson's telling of this story ends here, as he became too ill shortly afterwards to finish it. The poor chap lay at the door of the grim reaper for the next nine days, in and out of consciousness, finally succumbing to pneumonia on July 24th, 1929. It was quite early on that bright Wednesday evening that we said our final farewells. No Reichenbach turnabout this time, sad to relate.

Despite my protestations, Watson forced a diabolical commitment from me to finish off this tale of murder, identity theft and bank robberies, should he enter his blasted summerland before it was complete. This was something I had done before, albeit reluctantly, after his refusal to continue in the case involving the Notting Hill Rapist. I had also penned a couple of stories many years earlier, the names of which escape me at the moment. One of them had something to do with a lion, I believe.

'Why bother?' I asked him, as he lay, gaunt and skeletal beneath his beloved old army blanket. 'Most of the recent tales have been rejected by Strand magazine, and this one will probably suffer the same indignity. Predictably, your fickle readers have transferred their affections to the cosy and the country house murder story. Besides, we have heard nothing from those bank robbers since the incident of the travelling cats. Their trail has grown cold.'

Watson struggled to speak, but failed. His trembling hand motioned me to bend an ear down towards his blue-tinged lips.

'The ... truth. Must ... always tell ... the truth. About ... family,' he whispered, gripping my hand. 'Holmes ... best ... wisest.'

Then he collapsed back onto his pillow.

'Watson, my dear chap!' I murmured.

But he was gone.

I shall not trouble the reader with details of the deeply sorrowful feelings that were shared by Lily, Jasper and myself at the loss of our good companion. As I have said before, genuine grief must be endured by the individual. It is never shared between people, but merely spread around, like so much manure upon a fledgling rose-bed.

There followed a small funeral at Paddington Old Cemetery, most of his military and medical cohorts having already kicked the bucket, so to speak. Lily provided an early lunch at 221B for the few remaining colleagues who accepted her invitation. I declined, and spent the remainder of that morning in my sitting-room, smoking far too many pipes and pondering the speed at which Watson's heart had slowed down and ceased to beat, when his own doctor had predicted another few months of life. Although I had not indulged for quite a while, the thought of a seven-per-cent solution invaded my mind. Despite my doctor's orders.

I was glad I had withheld that one vital piece of information from my day's work at Somerset House. It would have broken him altogether if he'd discovered his mother had not, in fact, died when he was six. My enquiries proved that she had run off with Watson's birth father, Ormond Sacker and her daughter Jamie to the Old City of Jerusalem, where he was due to start preaching the gospel of Jesus in the Christ Church diocese. In his vain and wounded pride, Watson's adoptive father had lied to both children, and removed them to the far side of the world, thereby avoiding the chatter of his neighbours, relatives and friends.

My contemplation of that most loyal companion's troubled childhood was interrupted by a glimpse of the writing on the wall above his bed, courtesy of a sudden shaft of sunlight. And an equally sudden enlightenment.

'Stupid, stupid, STUPID! Bloody hell!'

Perhaps speaking aloud to myself was a sign of things to come, as I had just lost my faithful sounding board. There was noone to hear my muttered oath when I found myself staring at the letters from across the room. Now I saw an entirely different meaning to that word *Dieb*. It may very well be the German word for *thief.* Clever old Sherlock, eh? But what if the writer had been interrupted that night by Watson's waking up?

I grabbed a pen from the table and leapt across to the bed.

'*Die b.*' I filled in the remainder of the word. '*rother.*'

It was not a full stop at the end, merely the first dot of the letter *r*!

'*Die brother.*'

'We must exhume Watson immediately.'

About twenty pairs of startled eyes glared at the wild-eyed maniac who had burst into Lily's basement living room and made his announcement.

'But we've only just buried the man,' complained Canon Joshua Larchfield, an ascetic string bean of a fellow, whose memory of the Anglican funeral service had failed on at least three occasions during the morning.

'Watson was murdered by his twin sister.'

I directed this comment at Lestrade.

'Does it really matter?' asked a bloated grinning toad, who turned out to be Dr Francis Winston, Watson's own doctor, about whom he had complained vociferously in his last days. 'After all, he was dying anyway.'

Ignoring this fatuous comment, Lestrade inquired civilly as to how I had come to this conclusion. I then asked him to accompany me upstairs, where I clarified the proper meaning of the wall marking.

'He complained of a stiff neck the following morning,' I told the ferret-faced detective. 'I now believe Watson was poisoned in his bed that night, by an alkaloid which will be revealed in an autopsy. It may also provide a clue as to the whereabouts of his killer.'

'Mr Holmes. Let me be clear on this. Are you saying we need an autopsy *after* the corpse has been prepared for burial? And actually *buried*?'

'Yes. And as soon as possible. It is by no means unusual, in the case of a recent internment.'

Lestrade puffed out his cheeks as though he had never heard of such a thing and wanted to argue the point. But when I fixed him with my most baleful glare he began to reconsider, breathe properly again and come to the right decision.

'It will have to be tomorrow,' he muttered, glancing at his watch.

'Good man,' I replied. 'I would like my dear old friend to be tested for all known poisons. And I would also like to examine his neck afterwards.'

Needless to say, it was exactly as I had thought. The autopsy was carried out by a Scotland Yard pathologist at my request, in preference to Watson's useless physician. It proved the poison came from a type of snake known as *Cerastes cerastes*, commonly called the horned viper, to be found mainly in the deserts of North Africa and the

Middle East. My subsequent examination of Watson's neck showed two minute punctures to the skin, as though he had actually been bitten by a snake. I assumed he had not woken immediately due to the cocktail of drugs and sleeping tablets he was taking. This particular snake venom is not normally that toxic, but for a man who is already dying of cancer, it would result in damage to the lungs in the form of pneumonia and a concomitant slowing down of the heart rate until there is no rate at all. Oh, yes. Watson had most definitely been murdered. And murder is murder, even though the victim's days may already be numbered. But my satisfaction at this evidence was somewhat tainted by Lestrade's announcement later that evening, over a brandy administered by myself to calm down the trembling Scotland Yard detective.

'I am sorry to involve you in this case again, so soon after your colleague's death,' he spluttered. 'But there have been another *two* bank robberies, one in Hampstead and the other in Highgate. And they both took place at exactly the same time! 3.45 this afternoon! Fortunately noone was hurt. Yet both robbers left behind the *same* photo of the good doctor! And according to the tellers, both looked *just* like him! Like Dr. Watson in the picture!'

'Most interesting,' I mused. 'Identical twins of a fraternal twin, perhaps? But why the similarity to Watson? This case grows more fascinating by the day. Jasper, I believe it is now incumbent upon me to bring you up to date on the family history of my dear old friend. What I know of it, anyway.'

In the unlikely event that he was gazing down upon us from his summerland, I had to hope Watson would not begrudge my retelling of his childhood difficulties to the detective. Those early complications took a while to sink in, but he seemed to buck up soon afterwards, as though there was something solid to work with at last.

'It is a pity the Times newspaper does not keep records of people who ask for copies of their photos,' remarked Lestrade. 'The only other lead is the snake. Surely there cannot be that many horned vipers in the London area? I'll get my men onto the circuses, carnivals and theatres.'

'Also the streets. Look out for an act containing a snake-charmer and two identical strongmen. But Jasper, these people are clever. I doubt your men will find them. Meanwhile I shall spend the night meditating upon the peculiar sequence of events that constitute this case. Let me know how you get on tomorrow. Goodnight.'

As dawn broke, the only conclusion I had reached was that the absence of facts about the three people involved in Watson's murder, would necessitate the setting of a trap. When Lestrade also confirmed his predictible lack of success later on that evening, I sat him down at the table to outline my plan to bring Watson's killer to justice.

———————————

Watson's twin sister could not have been more unlike him physically. Instead of his tall, jolly shape, Jamie Sacker was petite and almost skeletally thin, as though she had been a ballet dancer all her life and not eaten in several days. Nevertheless, she seemed healthy enough, sitting upright in the bleak Scotland Yard interview room, across from Lestrade and myself. Once the snake had been removed from around her neck, I observed a pronounced goitre, signifying an enlarged thyroid gland. She was dressed in the standard Roma attire of spotted red scarf, white blouse, dull pleated calf-length skirt, flat shoes. Her talonesque nails were painted a familiar scarlet. Before speaking, she pulled a bent cigarette from some mysterious place within her blouse and lit it with a match offered by my colleague. The accent was brittle and tinged with faint echoes of the Scottish Highlands. But the voice was dead and her bitterness was evident from the start.

'What have you done with my boys, Hubert and Horace?' she demanded.

'They are in a cell down the corridor,' replied Lestrade. 'The pair will answer for the robberies and killing of the teller. You will be held for the murder of Dr. Watson.'

'Perhaps we should hear Miss Sacker's story before we go any further,' I suggested.

'Miss Sacker, hah! The great Sherlock Holmes has got straight to the point, as usual. You want to know why I asked my beautiful pet Jobi to bite your beloved friend and kill him, eh? My twin brother, the story-teller and retired army physician? Who had led such an interesting life? Well, maybe I'll tell you my story. But I warn you, it is not a pretty one. Not for the faint of heart.'

She drew deeply on her cigarette.

'My first six years of life were perfectly normal, apart from the absence of a real mother. My father, who was a vicar, told me that she had died when I was born. That she had gone to heaven. I believed him, being raised in the Anglican faith. Hah! Such a devout little girl, I was! We lived in a tiny village in Gloucester called Lower Slaughter. My nanny Dolly looked after me, and I remember those days as being very happy for me. Then suddenly everything changed. Another woman arrived on our doorstep, who said she was my mother. One day we were living in England, and almost immediately we were aboard this huge ship, which took many days to travel to a hot and humid city, which I came to know as Jerusalem. It was a confusing time for me, but I got to know my real mother on the trip, and soon forgot about Dolly and Little Slaughter. I had no idea of the existence of a twin brother at this time, or that she had been married to another man. This information was withheld from me by my mother, who was quite protective of me as I grew into a young woman.'

'Did they ever formally marry?' I enquired.

'No. They remained in a common law relationship. But I am getting ahead of my story.'

She threw her cigarette on the floor and ground it out.

'It was a quiet childhood, with my education provided by the nuns of St. Saviour's Convent School. I adjusted gradually to the heat and grew to enjoy its comforting warmth. There were only a few boys and girls of my age in the Christian compound beside the Jaffa Gate. Some were Jewish by tribe, but Christian by practice. This was still the Ottoman Empire, of course, so we were surrounded by Turks and Arabs, most of whom were Muslim, and did not mix socially with our families. You may find it difficult to believe, gentlemen, when you see this ancient wreck before you, with her withered features, that as a teenager, I was quite the most beautiful brown-skinned young girl in our neighbourhood, if not the whole of Jerusalem. It was when I reached my nineteenth birthday that disaster entered my life for the first of many times. May I have a glass of water, please?'

Lestrade duly obliged.

'I was an innocent young woman, without any education in matters of the flesh, so when my father entered my bedroom after a long day of celebration involving too much wine – he never drank alcohol, so any wine would have been too much, and he had been drinking all day – I assumed he was coming to give me my usual goodnight kiss. Instead of which, he climbed on top of me and ... violated me. Rape is the word used nowadays, I believe.'

'And incest is an additional crime,' sighed Lestrade.

She continued as though he had not spoken, taking a long draft of water.

'I did not understand what was happening at the time, as I knew nothing about men and their anatomy. I remember it as being an unpleasant and painful experience, with my drunken father giggling all the time and pretending that we were playing some kind of game. I did not tell my mother about this experience immediately, and the so-called Reverend Sacker went out of his way to avoid me afterwards. I believe he was ashamed, as well he should have been. Nobody knew about the incident until I started to feel unwell and my stomach swelled alarmingly. Even though I had stopped bleeding every month, I still had no idea what was happening until my mother noticed my morning sickness and guessed I was pregnant. She was furious, thinking I had gone with one of the local Arab boys or even worse, a Jew. At first, I had not the courage to inform on my father, as I was worried she would leave me behind with him in Jerusalem, and return alone to England.'

She paused to take another sip of water.

'Finally she broke down my resistance, and I told her the truth. Well! I am not sure that either of you nice-looking gentlemen can imagine a woman possessed of such incandescent rage. Fortunately I was not present when she confronted my father, but the very next day I was told to pack my belongings, and prepare for the boat trip back to England. The baby will be born there, and you are never again to have any further communication with that ... *creature*, she shouted at me. But despite his appalling action, I did not want to leave the only father I had ever known, so I threw an equally furious tantrum and tried to persuade her to remain somewhere nearby, if possible. Within travelling distance.'

Jamie Sacker drew another cigarette from within her blouse. Lestrade bent forward to light it for her.

'We settled upon Egypt and took a boat to Alexandria, followed by a train to Cairo. I remember being sick for most of the long journey, and worried about my unborn child.'

'What did you do for money?' asked Lestrade.

'My mother had threatened father with the exposure of his drunken deed to Bishop Gobat, which would have ended his career in the church. So we left with enough money to live on for many years. It was a very cheap part of the world, the Middle East, in those days. We rented a small villa on the outskirts of Cairo, in an area inhabited by expatriates, mainly British, and we made a home there. After the requisite time, imagine my surprise when, instead of one baby, out popped two identical little fellows from my swollen body, one after the other. It was a hellish experience, actually, but we shall not dwell upon such details, as I had my darlings Hubert and Horace, two names that my mother abhorred, incidentally. I was now a mother, like her, and she was only their grandparent.'

'Might I confirm the date of this event?' I enquired.

'May 10th, 1872.'

'So your twin sons are now fifty-seven years of age?'

'Indeed.'

'And the reason they look like Watson of twenty years ago, is because they shared a father with him? I just need to confirm that.'

'You haven't lost it, you know, Sherlock.'

Her sardonic smile was more of a grimace. 'Yes. They are my twin sons. Also my brothers. That was when my mother first explained to me about her lawful husband back in England. I discovered I had a twin brother named John Hamish, as well as an elder brother, Henry Hamish. She now deeply regretted having left Jack Watson after ten years of marriage and confessed that she should have insisted on keeping both twins with him. Instead she let me go with Ormond so that Henry could have a younger brother to play with. At this stage she had lost all contact with her old family. I leave you to work out the connections. It's complicated. Can I continue now?'

'Of course.'

'We lived together for ten years in Cairo until the next disaster. I had taken a part-time job as secretary to a local doctor from Pakistan. My mother had formed a new relationship with a certain Jack Hogan, who left her to return to England, without so much as a by your leave. She became seriously depressed, and one day I came back from work to find the two children playing in the garden, and my mother in the bath. A red bath. She had cut her wrists.'

'Dead?' Lestrade was clearly finding it difficult to cope with this litany of woes.

'As the proverbial doornail, Inspector. Did she get to heaven? Who knows? Me? I was thirty years of age with two identical children – to be honest there are still days

101

when I cannot tell Hubert from Horace – and a mother to bury. Whither Jamie Sacker?'

'Had you been in contact with your father during this time?' I asked.

'No. After my horrendous experience of childbirth, I changed my mind about wanting to see that man again. But when I telegraphed him in Jerusalem about my mother's suicide, I received a polite letter back from the Bishop stating that the Reverend Ormond Sacker had disappeared one day about six years earlier, with the wife of a local school-teacher. I have neither seen nor heard of my father since then.'

'I see. Do your children know their father is also their grandfather?' I asked.

'Hah! Well put, Sherlock! A mystery in itself. Indeed not. I explained to them that a man called John Hamish Watson was their father, who had left me before they were born. But I am getting ahead of my story again. When I investigated my mother's affairs, I discovered that all of the money we took with us from Jerusalem was gone. This may have contributed to her mood swings, I don't know. My part-time job was not enough to keep us going in the expatriate community, so I was faced with a decision. How could I pay the rent, raise my boys and provide them with the best possible education? I needed a second job. That was when I started my career as an illusionist.'

'Ah, the twins, of course!' I exclaimed.

'Leaping ahead as usual, Sherlock. Yes. I developed a stage act. I had always been fascinated by snakes, and it seemed I had some kind of empathy with them. So there were tricks with snakes and ropes, but the climax of the act was to make a young boy transport himself instantaneously from a cabinet on one side of the stage, to an empty one on the far side, leaving the first one empty. It was quite a novel magic trick for its time, although it is now routine. How did it work? Simply by having one twin drop down a trapdoor under the stage, and the other one spring up into the other cabinet.'

'But surely you were known to have identical twins?' queried Lestrade.

'Inspector, Cairo's population in 1882 was close to four hundred thousand, and as I have already stated, expatriates did not mix well with the indigenous population. Besides, during the summer months we joined a troupe and travelled around Egypt, performing in all the major cities. We became quite famous, actually. This lasted until the children finished school in 1890. Then another disaster arrived, in the shape of Hubert's broken leg, which happened when he had not prepared his landing cushion properly beneath the trapdoor. We had to leave the troupe and simultaneously our landlord in Cairo doubled the rent on our villa. I bought a caravan and a horse with the small amount of money I had left, and we departed from Egypt, to try our luck as travelling magicians, once Hubert's leg had healed. We called ourselves the Watsons.'

'Oh, and where did the Watsons travel to?' I enquired drily.

'For several years we headed west, along the coast through North Africa, passing through Tripoli, Tunis, Algeria and Morocco. But the going was hard. Money ran out, few people were interested in our tricks and before long we found ourselves destitute. And begging in these countries was not approved of. Fortunately, in 1897 I was still a handsome woman, and my children were good-looking boys. I need hardly draw a picture for you gentlemen to understand how we survived for another five years in a corrupt hell-hole like Morocco. But it was filth, pure filth!'

She banged her fists on the table at the memory.

'Prostit ...?' muttered Lestrade uneasily.

'Do please continue, madam,' I interrupted.

Jamie Sacker raised her head and stared through us and into an empty space, seeing only the next stage of her difficult life.

'We were desperate to get away from North Africa and into Europe. I suppose you might say that our lives as thieves began in Tangier, when I had an opportunity to steal enough money from one of my ... clients, as he lay exhausted and in a drug-fuelled stupor. This was 1902, by the way. The boys tied him up and gagged him, and we sailed on the first ship we could get for England and what I hoped would be a better life for us all. Perhaps one of you kind gents could spare a cigarette?'

Lestrade proffered his entire packet of Sullivans, along with a box of Vesta matches. His eyes were glazed and he looked slightly shell-shocked.

'Thank you. That's better.'

'Were you still doing your snake-charming act?' I asked.

'No. But little Jobi came with us nevertheless on the ship. I had made a serious mistake in thinking our vessel would be taking us to England. In fact, the captain was a thorough scoundrel who robbed us of the money we had already stolen, and dumped us near Calais. So there we were in France, without a single sou to our names and no knowledge of the language. You will forgive me if I had become a little cynical about human nature by this time, and fully prepared to do *anything* to keep myself and the twins alive. Having starved in Calais for three days, I introduced Jobi to a small boat owner, stole his food and sloop and set sail at midnight for Dover. But we never made it to England. Our sailing skills were non-existent. It was a nightmare. How we survived, I do not know.'

'But you obviously did,' I murmured.

'Yes. But only after a full week of more starvation, being tossed this way and that across a treacherous sea. When we pitched up on a beach, we could have been in the West Indies, for all I knew where we were.'

'Which was?'

'A small fishing village called Burnmouth, on the East Coast of Scotland. We had been buffeted over five hundred miles north, believe it or not. Fortunately, some Romani children noticed us on the seashore, and we were taken to a local campsite and looked after, as though we were part of the clan. When we recovered, I resolved to remain with those kind people and resurrect my magic act with Hubert and Horace. So we stayed with them for almost twenty-five years, the longest period of stability we had ever known, travelling all over Scotland and Northern England with their show. This was when I first became aware of the Strand Magazine, and the detective stories that featured the oh-so-clever Sherlock Holmes. Written by a certain Dr John H. Watson. I recognised the name, but could not be sure he was my twin brother. I read them all, and looked forward to the next one, just like everybody else. Later on I saw a wedding photo of him in a newspaper, and realised we must be related, due to his facial similarity to Hubert and Horace. I purchased the original and made copies of it, for no particular reason. This was twenty years ago, and I had no plans of ever meeting this happy-looking man.'

She paused to catch her breath before continuing.

'A couple of years ago, the Roma families were heading for Eastern Europe, so we split from them and made our way down to London, and yet more poverty. We were in the workhouse for a year, before deciding to start robbing banks to get some cash.'

'But if you had no money, why didn't you contact Watson?' I asked. 'He was a generous soul, and would not have been found wanting, once he had recovered from the shock of having a twin sister and two identical nephews. He only found out about you after the first Camden bank robbery. Your photo trick.'

'And why did you kill your twin brother, whom you had never even met?' Lestrade was also puzzled by her motive. 'Why that photo and the twin cats?'

'You did know he was dying of cancer anyway and had only a few months to live?' I queried. 'Otherwise your snake bite might not have killed him?'

She glared at me with narrowed eyes.

'Cancer? No, I did not. Hah! It would seem that we were twins in more ways than one. I too have cancer, a mere woman's version. It is also terminal. But don't worry. I'm sure I will live long enough to feel your rope around my neck. To answer your question. Because of my illness, I was filled with a sense of hopelessness and extreme jealousy of the life that he had lived.'

Her gaze softened.

'I could have been *your* friend, *your* old chap, *your* stormy petrel of crime in the extraordinary cases you have solved together. Instead I have been condemned to a life of sorrow, pain and despair. Of such seeds are hatred born. Hatred for my more fortunate twin brother. I believe he was even married a couple of times.'

'Oh, at least,' I replied.

She turned towards Lestrade, dead-eyed again.

'The cats were the ideas of my boys. They wanted to provide a puzzle for the great detective and his cohort, whom they believed to be the father who had abandoned them and their mother. Something that reflected them.'

'Twins.'

'Exactly. They carried the sculptures over to 221B Baker Street with me, and installed them while I used a key that your housekeeper had lost in order to enter, go upstairs with Jobi and put an end to his interesting life. I couldn't help leaving a message, even though it was incomplete, as he had woken up. Not such a great defence, is it?'

'No,' I replied. 'It is not a defence at all. But you would be mistaken if you believed Watson had led a completely happy life. He fought in a fearful war for his country, getting injured in two places, one of which remained with him for life. Both of his wives died. Unlike you, he never enjoyed the pleasure of having children. Plenty of people lead difficult lives, Miss Sacker. They do not all go around robbing banks and killing people. Lestrade, I believe we have heard enough, don't you?'

'Most definitely. Take her away, constable.'

As Watson's twin sister was being led from the room, she turned around to us and cackled: 'By the way, gents, you will have a job getting either Horace or Hubert to answer for the killing of the teller. In fact, you won't get any answer from them at all. You see, they are both deaf mutes, and have been since birth. And they don't understand common sign language. Only my own. I made sure of that. Who shot the bank clerk? They won't even tell *me*. God bless.'

It had been a simple plan that caught the trio in the end.

With Lily's help, Jasper and I disguised ourselves as beggars outside the two remaining banks in Hampstead and Highgate, ones that had not yet been robbed. I gave myself a twisted lip, inspired by one of our early cases. Jasper used some of his father's old clothes. All we had to do was keep a eye out for someone who looked like a younger Watson. It took several days, but eventually they turned up again at a synchronised time, entered the banks and robbed them at gunpoint without saying a word. It was a simple matter to cosh them both on their way out. Jamie Sacker was waiting for Hubert (or Horace) outside my bank, and ran screaming at the beggar who had laid out her son. It took little effort on my part to cosh her also, put a bullet in her damned snake and blow my whistle.

Yes, indeed. It was a simple plan. But it worked, and I felt a small sense of justice for my dear departed friend, who would never again take up his pen on my behalf.

Postscript:

I spent the following few months in a state that others might call grief, but which I would categorise as a profound contemplation of my future. After many pipes, I decided finally to return to the cottage in Cuckmere Haven. I hope to be settled back on the Sussex Downs in time for Christmas. I shall not be keeping an apiary this time. I may study to become a carpenter, or something creative like that. I really don't know yet. At seventy-five, I may be too old for such activities. Now that my brother and colleague are gone, I find little to keep me in London. All of the more interesting cases make their way onto the desks of Lord Peter Wimpsey and that greasy Belgian, Hercule Pottyrot (with his horrible moustache and little grey cells), in spite of my close association with Jasper Lestrade.

He and his wife Lily have protested their deepest concern at my departure, and how much they will miss me, etcetera, etcetera, but I sense their barely suppressed desire to occupy the rooms on the second and third floors of 221B Baker Street, especially now that Lily is expecting another noisy little monster to run around the place.

Watson's murderous twin sister, Jamie, duly met her comeuppance at the end of a rope, singing an obscure Protestant hymn all the way to the scaffold. Her two deaf mute sons were sent to the Hanwell Asylum for life, as noone could find a way of communicating with them, to establish exactly which one had killed the bank teller. Weaving baskets should continue to keep them quiet. Just desserts, I say.

As I was going through Watson's few remaining possessions, I discovered a harrowing tale about a kidnapper in Kensington at the bottom of a suitcase. The events took place shortly after his second marriage to Beatrice in late 1902, and before my first decampment to the Sussex Downs. Unusually for those heady days of our wide readership, the story was marked as having been rejected for publication by the Strand magazine. Perhaps this was the reason it had not found its way into his tin dispatch-box in Cox & Company of Charing Cross.

Out of respect for my old comrade, I now submit it yet again to that same august publication, with the hope that a more enlightened audience in 1929 may not be so offended by its grisly contents.

15. Sherlock Holmes And The Kensington Kidnapper.

'Mrs Hudson! MRS HUDSON! Where in damnation is the bloody woman?'

'She probably heard you the first time,' I commented mildly.

'But she has not appeared since lighting the fire this morning! I have had to build it up myself,' complained Holmes, sprawling indolently across the cane sofa and threading a pipe-cleaner through the shank of his cherrywood.

'Normally she is like an aged gazelle up those stairs, keen to supply my every want. You will have tea, won't you, Watson? I assume your visit is not purely social, and am aware your afternoon tea is a precious ritual, which I could not persuade you to abandon before you made the selfish mistake of marrying for a second time. Once is forgiveable, but twice is wishful thinking on your part, old chap. And you have put on yet another seven and a half pounds, unless I am mistaken.'

My heart filled with warmth at the mention of my altered status in life. Contrary to my friend's cynical comment, my new wife Beatrice and I, having been married for over a month, were as content as any two people could be. It was November 6th, 1902, and we had just returned from a long honeymoon in the Seychelles. I had braved the dense fog, a real London peculiar, to visit Holmes at 221B Baker Street and see how he was faring without me as his companion. Not too well, it seemed. His mood suggested a recent injection of some narcotic or other.

'I am so thoroughly bored, Watson,' he said, blowing through the bit of his pipe into the hissing fire to clear out the stem. 'There is no scientific subject worth investigating that I have not examined thoroughly. My violin tempts me not. Especially now that you aren't here to appreciate it. Crime in London is at an all time low. There has been nothing of interest since the Red Circle business. I even find myself wishing Jack would make a return to the streets. You know me. I cannot live without brain-work. I abhor the dull routine of existence. My mind rebels at stagnation. I *crave* for mental exaltation. Mrs Hudson! MRS HUDSON!'

'This must be her now, Holmes.'

I had heard the patter of feet upon the stairs. But it was not the landlady's stately tread, merely Billy the page, who knocked timidly on the sitting room door before entering with a silver platter, upon which lay a single cream envelope.

'This letter came for you, sir,' he said, handing the plate to my friend, who lifted the envelope delicately between two fingers.

'Wait,' he commanded Billy, as he pulled a penknife from a pocket, inserted it lazily into the sleeve, slit the wrapper open and extracted a sheet of paper. He held it up to the light as he read it.

'Hmmm. That explains it,' he muttered, handing the paper to me.

I tried to make sense of the note, but failed dismally:

'I veha uryo rsm hounds. Fi uyo natw ot ese rhe levia gnaai, ti lilw stoc oyu neo handouts nudsop ni desu oenst. Velae het scha nidhbe eth xwa rugfei fo Yprec Roefly Opntmale ni Demmaa Duusssat ta etn ma ooowrrtm. Fi yuo od ton, rrappee ot teg neo fo ruyo eeeeprkssohu ydbo

112

tsarp ni eht txne stpo, nda treoahn neo ni chae stpo hrafttreee. Gnides, A. Ragman.'

'All right, Sherlock Holmes. This is nonsense to me. Do your thing. What does it mean?' I sighed.

'Anagrams,' he replied sniffily. 'Childish, really. Even the puzzles are tedious nowadays. Always assuming the author is not dyslexic, of course.'

I perused the note again, with this vital clue to the simplicity of its code:

'I have your Mrs Hudson. If you want to see her alive again, it will cost you one ...'

'Thousand,' interjected Holmes.

'... thousand pounds in used notes. Leave the cash behind the wax figure of ...'

'Percy Lefroy Mapleton. He was a journalist who murdered a coin-dealer on a train in 1881. His was the first police composite picture ever to appear in a newspaper.'

'... Percy Lefroy Mapleton in ...'

'Madame Tussauds. Really, Watson! Do make an effort! Our friend Percival resides in the Chamber Of Horrors, by the way.'

'... Madame Tussauds at ten am tomorrow. If you do not, prepare to get one of your ...'

'Housekeeper's.'

'... housekeeper's body parts in the next post, and another one in each post thereafter. Signed, A. Ragman.'

'Which, as I'm sure you know, is itself an anagram of the word anagram. Our kidnapper has a sense of humour. Unless, of course, he has been foolish enough to provide us with his real name. Billy, can you tell us when Mrs Hudson went out, or if she had any visitors today?'

'I don't know, sir. She was definitely downstairs at about ten this morning, to let me in. I was busy all day, bringing in the coal and polishing the brasses. As far as I know, nobody called, except for the person who dropped that letter through the slot.'

'Right. And I had told her not to bring me any food. Thank you, Billy. You may go.'

'But ... but, this is terrible! Mrs Hudson has been kidnapped!' I expostulated. 'He is threatening to cut her up! We must *do* something!'

The great detective lounged even further down into the sofa and murmured, 'He *or* she. Watson, I wonder if you can lay your hands upon a thousand pounds?'

'Holmes!' I cried, leaping from my chair in agitation. 'You don't mean to tell me you intend to *pay* this ransom? Aren't you going to examine the message, envelope and paper for clues? Find out when that poor long-suffering woman left the building, and if anyone in the street saw her? Use your skills to rescue her and catch the foul kidnapper? This is the very crime you have been waiting for! And shouldn't we call Inspector Lestrade?'

His only response was to yawn widely.

'And what are you going to do about eating, for heaven's sake?' I continued.

'Oh, I ate last week.' He smiled weakly at the old joke.

'We must work on it together,' I decided, sitting down again, determined to shake him out of his torpor.

'But surely you will be wanting to get back to your connubial bliss with all possible haste,' he suggested slyly.

'I shall explain everything to Beatrice and she will understand. My wife is a very understanding woman. She will want me to be involved, with a person's life at stake.

Very well. If you will not, then I shall hide in the Wax Museum tomorrow at ten with my Bulldog and capture this filthy crook when he or *she* comes looking for the money. Poor Mrs Hudson! And no. I certainly cannot find a thousand pounds at such short notice, since you ask. Holmes! Good God, man! Wake up!'

But he had fallen fast asleep, dead to the world and to no amount of shaking.

I kept my word. Yet when I arrived at 221B Baker Street the following morning, hoping to persuade my friend to accompany me to Madame Tussauds, there was noone to be found. I assumed that Holmes had recovered from his self-abuse and gone out for breakfast somewhere. Beatrice had given me her heartfelt imprimatur the night before, to do whatever it took (her words) to find Mrs Hudson, but to take great care of myself. She had no desire to become a widow, just yet. Oh, how I do enjoy my dear wife's sense of humour!

I checked my service revolver for bullets, made sure the safety catch was off, limped through the fog of Baker Street to the Marylebone Road and turned left past the Underground Station towards the Wax Museum. I was carrying a bag of newspaper clippings Beatrice and I had cut up. Hopefully it resembled a thousand pounds in used notes.

It was just as well I'd given myself plenty of time. There was already a significant queue and I had to take my place patiently, hoping I could get into the Chamber Of Horrors by ten o'clock. The peasouper was just beginning to raise its gloom while the line of people moved ahead at a snail's pace towards the entrance. It occurred to me the kidnapper himself might also be waiting to gain access to the Museum, so I kept my eyes peeled for any shifty-looking characters, with one hand in readiness upon my pistol.

I need not have worried so much, as I was inside Madame Tussauds by 9:50am, and following the crowd on their way down to the creepy Chamber Of Horrors, by far the most popular attraction. This secret room was dimly-lit and filled with a cloying mist that made me want to sneeze. My idea was to place the bag behind the waxwork of this Mapleton chap and linger nearby to see who arrived to take it. Fortunately Percy Lefroy did not attract nearly as much attention as the two body snatchers, Burke and Hare.

I had little difficulty in slipping the cuttings behind the wax figure of the slouching chinless murderer. The poster beside it informed the reader that an incompetent detective called Sergeant Holmes had been involved in his capture! I grinned to myself. A distant relation, perhaps?

'No.'

I swung around to see where that voice had come from. It sounded just like my old friend, reading my mind as usual. But there was noone there! The nearest wax figure to Mapleton was James Bloomfield Rush, the notorious murderer of his landlord, Isaac Jermy and his son, also Isaac Jermy, when the Rush farm's mortgage had run out. Then I noticed the shadow in the corner of the room, supposed to represent Jack the Ripper, whose physical appearance was unknown and therefore had no wax image, merely an upright wooden board, painted black. It would make a perfect hiding place. Keeping my finger cocked on the trigger of my revolver, I decided to take a closer look behind this cloaked black shadow. And found another shadow.

'Holmes! It's you,' I whispered, when I recognised his familar languid shape lying against the wall behind Jack's figure. 'Great minds think alike.'

'And fools seldom differ. Did you bring the money?'

I explained the subterfuge that Beatrice and I had planned, in the full expectation of capturing the kidnapper, or his representative. With the two of us there, we would be sure to overcome any criminal. All I had to do was sit down beside my friend and wait.

And wait. And wait. And wait. After four hours of nobody showing the slightest interest in old Percy, my stomach was grumbling that it was well past time for a bite of lunch. Disappointed, we agreed to alternate the remaining five hours in one-hour shifts until the Museum closed at 7pm, so that we could smoke a pipe or two. Then we would meet up later on at 221B Baker Street.

But nobody came for the clippings. Holmes had to bring the bag back with him, to await further instructions. Which were readily available in the form of a small brown cardboard box, tied by a crossed string and left on the steps of his lodgings. Fearing the worst, and still suffering from the after effects of his recent binge, the great detective did not touch it until I had arrived, and was sharing a bottle of his best Hennessy.

'You open it, old fellow,' he said. 'After all, you are the surgeon.'

'*Was*. Oh, very well,' I replied, snipping the string with my penknife. 'But I am sure it is not as bad as you think.'

I was wrong. It was.

'What is it?' demanded Holmes, as I held up a bloody pulp of glistening flesh with my penknife.

'A tongue,' I replied grimly. 'A human tongue. Recently detached from its owner, I believe.'

'But not necessarily Mrs Hudson's,' he stated flatly.

Wonder of wonders. At last he seemed to be getting interested in the case of his missing landlady.

'It looks far too fresh for such a talkative middle-aged woman. And it has been cut by a kitchen knife with a serrated edge. Most interesting. Is there a message with it?'

I turned the box upside down and around, but could find nothing in the way of writing anywhere. Not even an anagram or two. The bottom was about to fall open from the quantity of blood that had seeped through it.

Holmes peered inside.

'There is an outer layer to the cardboard, Watson. Pull it out and we might find another missive.'

As usual, he was right. It was pencilled around the inside of the outer layer of cardboard. But it did not look like more anagrams to me:

'Hvftt xibu! Op cbol xjmm bddfqu ofxtqbqfs dmjqqjoht bt dbti! Boe opx zpvs ipvtflffqfs xjmm ofwfs tqfbl bhbjo. Zpvs gbvmu. Cvu J xjmm gpshjwf uijt njtublf, qspwjefe zpv mfbwf uxp uipvtboe qpvoet cfijoe uif jotfdu ipvtf jo Mpoepo A pp bu oppo upnpsspx. B. Sbhnbo.'

'Oh, gosh. More gobbledygook,' I muttered. 'No doubt you have broken the code already?'

'Indeed,' replied Holmes serenely. 'It is a simple alphabetic adjustment of one place to the right each time. So A becomes B, B becomes C, etcetera, etcetera, right down to Z becoming A. Our kidnapper might be a child. Or a satirical adult, who is apparently looking for more money.'

'You had better read it out to me,' I sighed.

'*Guess what! No bank will accept newspaper clippings as cash! And now your housekeeper will never speak again. Your fault. But I will forgive this mistake, provided you leave two thousand pounds behind the insect house in London Zoo at noon tomorrow. A. Ragman.*'

'How in hell did he find out about the paper clippings?' I asked.

'That is a very good question, Watson. Eh, just how well do you know your new wife?'

'Holmes! I do not care for your suggestion!'

'Calm down. Only you and I and that good lady know the bag is full of newspaper cuttings. It was not touched in the Museum. I told noone and I presume the same of you. Ergo ...?'

'I suggest we leave my wife out of this case from now on,' I responded coldly.

'Very well,' muttered Holmes. 'It must remain a mystery for the time being. I shall transfer the clippings to a different bag, add another bunch to it and keep it here overnight. Why don't we meet at the insect house at 11.45am?'

'Agreed. And now I shall bid you good *night*.'

I was so incensed by Holmes' remark about Beatrice that I almost did not travel to the Zoological Gardens the following morning. Only my consideration for the plight of Mrs Hudson led me to make the journey through the dense fog to the insect house. Unfortunately there had been a traffic accident along the way involving a pair of those cursed experimental motor buses. My growler was delayed by ten minutes, so when I arrived at twelve sharp the enlarged bag was already leaning against the wall behind the insect house, with the great detective sitting on a bench beside it, smoking a cigarette and reading The Times.

'Morning, Holmes.'

'Ah, Watson. There you are. No luck yet, I'm afraid.'

'Eh, perhaps we should place ourselves out of sight?' I suggested.

'Splendid notion!' he agreed, rolling up his newspaper. 'I was waiting for you to show up. We'll hide in the insect house and keep an eye on things through one of the windows.'

'All right. I suppose so.'

My hatred of all things creepy and crawly had begun many years earlier in the desert of Afghanistan. Although they had not been directly responsible for the bout of enteric fever that ended my military career, I had treated many fellow soldiers for vectorborne diseases such as malaria and dengue fever and witnessed at first hand the devastation that flying insects can wreck upon the human frame. Fortunately the London Zoo's collections of bugs were safely contained within their individual glass chambers. I did not even have to look at the disgusting creatures as we settled ourselves behind a window to the rear of the empty insect house.

This time we did not have long to wait. Five minutes or so had passed before I heard a faint rustling outside. Someone was handling the bag of clippings! I peered through the window. A bowler-hatted, well-dressed gentleman of middle years with a grey Van Dyke beard underneath a pair of black pince-nez was tucking the bag under his arm. He looked around briefly, turned on his heel and ambled away with a slight roll to his gait. I had grabbed my pistol and was about to slip out to challenge the kidnapper, when Holmes pulled me back and hissed into my ear.

'Let him take the bag. We can follow. Our friend might bring us to Mrs Hudson. Just wait for a few seconds. Then you go first, old chap. I'll be close behind you.'

'Right.'

The damned blighter was whistling away to himself and swinging the bag backwards and forwards with his right hand as I shadowed him from about thirty yards. There were plenty of people on the path through the Zoo, so I had no worries about being discovered, especially as the fog had not yet lifted. Some elephants trumpeted in the distance. A series of answering roars echoed across the open grass from the lion house.

I glanced behind to locate my friend, but could see no sign of him. This was a big mistake, as when I turned around again, my quarry had also vanished into the mist! I limped forward as quickly as I could, scanning the paths in front and to the sides, but it was no good.

I spent the next hour searching the grounds of the Zoo, again without success. I had to accept that I'd lost the damned kidnapper. What on earth would Holmes say?

'Not to worry, old fellow. I had quite anticipated that he would lose you. Which is why I followed him myself.'

'But how? I could not see you anywhere.'

After a brief lunch, I had returned to 221B Baker Street, prepared to apologise for my failure and eat the vast quantities of humble pie that were the norm in situations like this. I found Holmes seated calmly in front of a roaring fire, enjoying a cigar and continuing his journey through The Times.

'Ah, yes. But could you see *this* person?'

He placed the newspaper over his head, fiddled around with something from the sofa, pulled the crumpled Times back down, and displayed the visage of a bespectacled, black-bearded Orthodox Jew, complete with yarmulke and a small tallit, or prayer shawl. He was totally unrecognisable.

'I remember you now! You overtook me and raced ahead, muttering away to yourself. But where did you get the disguise?'

'As you know, I keep various camouflages hidden in secret hideaways around London,' he replied, obviously enjoying his deceit. 'This one is normally to be found inside the Ready Money Drinking Fountain in Regent's Park. If you shift one of the four square blocks at its base in a south-easterly direction, the hidey-hole is revealed.'

I sat down beside him and took out my pipe.

'I suppose you were quoting some Hebrew prayer as you went along, for the sake of verisimilitude?'

'*Barukh ata Adonai Eloheinu, melekh ha'olam, asher kid'shanu b'mitzvotav v'tzivanu l'hit'atef ba'tzitzit,*' intoned the great detective.

'Good grief! That sounds like one of the kidnapper's messages.'

'*Blessed are YOU, LORD our GOD, King of the universe, Who has sanctified us with His commandments and has commanded us to wrap ourselves with fringes.* It is usually spoken before putting on this shawl. I kept repeating it.'

By this time my pipe was drawing nicely.

'I won't ask how you could know such a thing, Holmes. But you must tell me where this scoundrel went, and whether we are any nearer to finding the excellent Mrs Hudson.'

His reply was to remove the disguise and lift up the bag of newspaper clippings from behind the cane sofa. He released the knot and extricated a large package wrapped in brown paper, which he placed on the sofa beside me.

'Alas, I do not know. I too lost him in the fog. We must accept the fact that our enemy has been one step ahead of us at every stage. Open it.'

'Certainly not. It's your turn. Where did you find it?'

'In a bin at the entrance to the Zoo. He had obviously anticipated our continued deception and planned the whole thing in advance. I suspect the package will contain another body part and an equally juvenile message. With more money required. We may have to pay him off this time. He is playing games with us. Go on. Open it.'

'No.'

'Oh, Watson, you are such a stubborn mule! All right! Here goes!'

Holmes cut through the brown paper with his penknife, revealing another envelope, clasped by a discoloured human hand, severed at the wrist.

'Excellent,' he said. 'No blood this time. The smoothness at the wrist shows that this female paw has clearly been sawn off well after death. Yet it contains Mrs Hudson's wedding ring. Most interesting. Now what are his latest instructions?'

Holmes had to wriggle the envelope out of the hand's rigorous grip. Once he'd opened it and pulled out a sheet of paper, he read the contents to himself and handed it over to me:

'namgaR .A .daeh a niatnoc lliw lecrap txen eht ,noonretfa worromot mp00.1 yltcaxe ta ereht yenom eht

123

*dnif ton od I fI .retniw eht gnirud tpek si ti erehw wonk
lliw nostaW rotcoD .dnuorG tekcirC s'droL ta rellor
yvaeh eht htaenrednu detisoped eb ot – repap ton ,sdnuop
– sdnuop dnasuoht eerht tnaw won I .ydob reh fo strap
repeekesuoh ruoy dna yenom uoy gnitsoc si yaled ruoY
.deyonna yllaer gnitteg ma I woN.'*

'Ok. No. Don't tell me, Holmes,' I cried. 'I understand
it. The message is backwards. Not much of a coding
system this time, thank heavens. I can even read it
myself:'

*'Now ... I am ... getting really ... annoyed. Your delay
is ... costing you ... money and your ... housekeeper parts
of her body. I now want three ... thousand pounds – ...
pounds, not paper – to be ... deposited underneath the
heavy ... roller at Lord's Cricket Ground. Doctor Watson
will know where it is kept during the ... winter. If I do not
find the money there at ... exactly 1.00pm tomorrow ...
afternoon, the next parcel will contain a ... head. A.
Ragman.'*

'Surely now is the time to call in Lestrade, don't you
think, Holmes? Scotland Yard have the resources. They
would be more capable of risking three thousand pounds
than either of us.'

The great detective shook his head.

'Lestrade will only get in the way, as per usual. Mrs
Hudson is *my* housekeeper now, so I shall pay a visit to
the bank this afternoon, and withdraw the required
money. But I have no intention of relinquishing it. I shall
use it to entrap this fellow. I have also sent a telegram to
Mycroft, arranging to meet him at the Diogenes Club
later on this afternoon. It is my hope that he will be of
assistance to us in defeating our foe.'

'But do you know who he is?' I demanded.

'Not yet. I need more facts. At the moment I am fumbling in the dark. You know my methods, Watson. Here is a question for you. Assuming that Mrs Hudson is still alive and unmarked, what kind of people would have access to spare body parts, so they could pretend to be cutting her up in order to blackmail us?'

'Doctors. Nurses. Mortuary attendants. Pathologists. Grave robbers,' I replied. 'And of course, murderers.'

Holmes blew a faultless smoke ring towards the ceiling.

'But the nature of the coded messages might suggest an immature mind. Someone young, perhaps?'

'A student of medicine?'

'Exactly!'

'But the man at the Zoo was middle-aged! And he looked quite ... well-off.'

'He might also have been disguised. Or there may be more than one person in this game. We shall soon find out.'

Holmes stood up abruptly.

'And now, old fellow, if you don't mind, I must make that trip to the bank.'

'Would you like me to come with you?' I asked.

'That won't be necessary,' he replied, pulling on his Ulster.

'You could then dine with us afterwards?' I suggested, as we descended the seventeen stairs to the hall.

'Thank you, Watson. I have already booked Simpsons-In-The-Strand for every evening until Mrs Hudson's return. Tonight's menu includes roast rib of beef with Yorkshire pudding. One of your favourites, I believe? However, do give my best regards to your fragrant new wife. I shall meet you at the St John's Wood Road entrance to Lord's tomorrow at 12.45pm. Toodle-pip!'

And a toodle to your pip, too. I must admit that I was quite jealous of his roast beef that evening. When I returned home, my darling Beatrice had prepared a delicious raw salad of beetroot, asparagus, artichokes, spinach and beans, washed down by elderflower cordial. I went to bed feeling quite bloated, and not a little cheated.

As it happens, I did not meet my friend at the home of cricket the following day. He arrived on our doorstep at ten minutes past eight, in a state of high excitement, just as I was preparing to put in a few hours at my medical practice in Paddington. He looked quite exhausted and had obviously not attended to his toilet that morning.

'I have found him, Watson!' he cried. 'Hurry up! We must go at once. That cab over there is ours.'

'Who? Where?'

'Why, our kidnapping blackmailer, of course! We are going to his home at 27 Scarsdale Villas in Kensington! Quick, man! It has all been naught but a game until now! We have to get there before he chops off poor Mrs Hudson's head! But we may be too late already! Bring your Bulldog! And many bullets!'

Once he had calmed down somewhat, Holmes explained his findings to me on the way to our destination.

'You may have perceived a certain levity in my attitude towards this kidnapping caper up until now, Watson.'

'It has been quite noticeable,' I replied.

'Truthfully, this case has not exercised my mind greatly. At first I thought Mrs Hudson herself was behind the staging of her own kidnapping, in an attempt to provide me with an interesting, if rather gruesome case. Just to keep me occupied, so to speak. The childish codes, the tongue and the hand with her ring so obviously placed upon it.'

'But she would never do such a thing!' I cried.

Holmes leaned forward and steepled his fingers beneath his chin.

'Indeed. Where would she get a spare tongue or a hand, for instance? It was while I was at the bank, collecting the money, that a more devious explanation occurred to me. What if our blackmailing friend *wanted* us to believe that this was a staged kidnapping, complete with its simplistic puzzles? In order to put us off the scent, so that we would not take it seriously enough when he came to implement his *real* plan?'

'Which is?'

'The murder of our landlady, of course. Suppose he guessed that we would only supply newspaper clippings at Madame Tussaud's, and did not even have to appear there? And he obviously anticipated a repeat performance at the Zoo.'

'But he did turn up,' I argued. 'He cannot have been sure that he would give us the slip then.'

'Yes. That was a risk he took, to continue his game. But the stakes are high, Watson. Let me explain. After my trip to the bank, it occurred to me that the key to this case lay in Mrs Hudson's past life, about which I knew precious little. So I visited her sister, Mabel, at home in Fulham. She insisted upon a tedious afternoon tea with disgusting cakes and biscuits before I had a chance to open my mouth. And her smelly brat Emily crawled around my legs like a dog looking for a tree to urinate against. But eventually I discovered what I wanted to know.'

'Which was?'

Holmes reclined upon his seat.

'You and I had always assumed that Mrs Hudson was a widow, did we not?'

'Yes,' I replied. 'She told me once that her husband had been killed fighting the Boers in Africa.'

'Not so. Perhaps the truth was an embarrassment to her. Mable confirmed that her sister had actually divorced an alcoholic husband, gaining 221B Baker Street to live in as her settlement, with rooms to rent as an income. The man's name is Morse Hudson and he is a disgraced pathologist, who was subsequently forced to flee the country for Canada to avoid prosecution. Apparently the swine had conducted a bungled autopsy on a prostitute while the worse for drink and singing *'The Old Chisolm Trail'*. She was the third of Jack The Ripper's victims – Elizabeth Stride. By the time he was finished with her, the police had nothing left but a skeleton to work with.'

'So you think he has returned to London with vengeance on his mind?' I asked.

'Not vengeance, Watson. Our old friend, filthy lucre. Not just my money, either. That would be a mere bonus to him. Mable told me that Mrs Hudson had agreed as part of her divorce arrangement, that 221B Baker Street would revert to the ex-husband in the event of her death. I believe that he has returned from Canada in order to murder her, regain the property and sell it on. Now that the fuss about Jack has died down, and more than a decade has passed, he probably feels safe from the law. If it were not for a possible interference by his ex-wife's famous detective tenant, that is.'

'But how did you discover where he lives?'

Holmes laughed. To himself, admittedly.

'Mycroft, of course. He was not best pleased to have received my telegram. I disturbed his snooze when I arrived at the Diogenes Club. We had to go into the Stranger's Room, where I demanded his help in the strongest terms. At first he was reluctant to use his brain and those famous political connections of his in a situation which did not directly threaten the state. But he capitulated when I told him that he would be forced to see a lot more of his younger brother if Mrs Hudson could not be found, safe and well. Maybe even have to live with him. That certainly concentrated his mind!'

'I can imagine,' I said.

I could not help smiling at the thought of the two brothers living together. The exhausting daily competitions to see who was the cleverest. Mycroft wanting food all the time, and the ascetic Sherlock avoiding it as much as possible. The angry silences. It would never work.

'I asked him to trace the movements of a certain pathologist called Morse Hudson, from the time of his scarpering to Canada fourteen years ago, until now. As you know, Mycroft's tentacles spread all around the world, not just the United Kingdom. He was able to use the newly-installed Post Office telephone exchange – far more efficient than the telegram, old chap, believe me – to make two calls from the Diogenes Club. Without having to move from his seat! He refused to clarify whom he was connecting to, but hearing him talk on this new device led me to consider the plight of the criminal in the future. I feel that crime will cease to exist, now that the police force is able to unite against it across the planet. We are about to become redundant, Watson!'

'Oh, I doubt that, Holmes. Surely the crooks will also be able to communicate more quickly, and outfox the law that way?'

Holmes shrugged.

'Perhaps, if they can afford one of the things. Damned expensive at the moment, they are. When he had finished his calls, Mycroft explained to me that it would take him several hours to gather the information I needed, and there was no point in my waiting around. I could see he wanted to return to his nap, so I offered to send Billy around to his office in Whitehall first thing this morning. He demurred and said a telegram would have to do. I agreed, and returned to 221B Baker Street, fully intending to relax and dine out at Simpson's. But I grew progressively more agitated by the possibility of finding Mrs Hudson's head in a bag by the heavy roller at Lord's the following morning. So I had to take a little ... something to get me through the night.'

'I thought so. Cocaine?' I enquired. 'You know that drug will do for you in the end, Holmes.'

'Morphine. It quite knocked me out. I woke up at seven this morning on the floor of the sitting-room. Mycroft's telegram arrived within the hour, and I hurried over to seek your help. Oh, look. Here we are at Scarsdale Villas.'

Holmes thumped the roof of the cab with his cane.

'Thank you, cabbie. This will do nicely. Please wait for us. Hudson is occupying the basement apartment. Come, Watson. The game is most definitely afoot!'

As, indeed, was the London fog. We threaded our way slowly across the road towards a rickety wooden gate, almost completely hidden by an overgrown hedge. My Bulldog was gripped firmly in my hand as I followed Holmes through the wicket and down several steps.

'No need for diplomacy, I believe,' he said, banging his cane firmly on the door.

A few minutes passed before it was opened slightly by the very same person who had collected the bag from the Zoo, beard and all, but minus the pince-nez. I raised my revolver.

'Is this a burglary?' he asked innocently.

Holmes ignored his question.

'Are you Morse Hudson?' he demanded sternly.

'Yes. Who might you be?'

'My name is Sherlock Holmes and the person covering you with his pistol is Dr. Watson.'

'Ah. I see,' he said. 'You have found me. How clever of you. Won't you come in?'

He stepped aside politely to let us in, but just as I had crossed the threshold after Holmes and followed him into a dank kitchen, the pathologist ran out the front door, pulling it shut. He held onto the handle from the outside. I was just about to shoot him through the glass, when he let go abruptly and vanished up the steps. Opening the door, I limped after him. He turned around at the gate and lifted something like a football from behind his back.

'Here, catch!'

He threw the thing at me, knocking the gun from my hand, and disappeared down the road into the fog.

'Don't worry, Watson. I'll get him.'

Holmes shot up the steps and after the villain like a bullet.

Picking up my gun, I took a closer look at Hudson's missile. And almost fainted. It was a human head! Some poor woman's! Her mouth was open and lacking any sign of a tongue. The crook must have been holding it by the hair behind his back. I had to examine the horrible object closely to verify that it could never have belonged to dear old Mrs Hudson. The features were far too young, and bore no resemblance to Holmes' housekeeper. Her thin lips were fixed in a rictus grin and her hair, though matted with dried blood, was clearly blonde, not grey. Thankfully, the eyes were closed.

I breathed a huge sigh of relief.

Even in my army days in Afghanistan, I had never held a human head in my hand, so I disposed of it swiftly in the kitchen and set about searching the apartment for Mrs Hudson. But I did not find her. What I did find were the remains of this unfortunate woman, who was missing both a hand and a head. Her naked corpse was lying on a bed to the rear of the flat, behind a small sitting room. I had never seen a sadder sight. Recovering the head, I placed a sheet delicately over the poor dismembered creature.

Now where in blue blazes was Mrs Hudson?

I decided to wait patiently for Holmes in the kitchen, while trying to apply his methods to the problem. Needless to say, I was failing dismally at this when the front door clattered open and he appeared behind the whimpering figure of Morse Hudson, whom he was holding up by the collar of his shirt.

'Let ... me ... go,' grunted the pathologist.

'Certainly,' replied Holmes, flinging him onto a chair by the stove. 'One move out of you, and my friend will shoot. Isn't that right, Watson?'

I withdrew my pistol and trained it firmly on Hudson. Then I explained to Holmes what I had found in the bedroom. He was greatly relieved that the body did not belong to Mrs Hudson.

'Have you searched the place thoroughly?' he asked.

'Yes. All cupboards, wardrobes and recesses. No secret hidey-holes. The small garden to the rear is overgrown with weeds. There does not seem to have been any recent digging. She is not here.'

Holmes sat down opposite Hudson and poked him in the belly with his stick.

'Well? What about it, you murderous little worm? What have you done with my housekeeper? Answer me! Or I shall give you a taste of my cane!'

The pathologist sat up in his chair, straightened his shirt and patted his hair back into place. It was an affort at dignity that was at odds with the fear in his eyes. For the first time I noticed how pale, exhausted and gaunt he looked, beneath his Van Dyke beard, all sure signs of a love affair with John Barleycorn.

'I ... I ... how dare ... oh, Christ! All right! The game is surely up now. In truth, I have had enough anyway. My *darling* ex-wife Martha Hudson is in St Barts hospital, in a coma. Unfortunately I did not finish off the nasty money-grabbing cow!'

'What happened?' demanded Holmes. 'And calm down, or it will go worse for you.'

There was another attempt at nobility on the part of our captive, complete with a royal shake of the head, but it also failed.

'I was once a respected pathologist, you know,' he whined. 'Scotland Yard depended on my work as evidence in serious crimes. Including those infamous Jack The Ripper murders!'

He started to weep.

'We know all about that, and your enforced departure to Canada due to drink and incompetence,' stated Holmes flatly. 'When did you return? And why?'

'I had to come back,' he sniffed. 'There were no opportunities for a man of my talents in Canada, without the proper references. I spent twelve years of my life working as a mortuary attendant in Toronto, for a piddling wage. Even that came to an end eventually and I decided to return to London and take my chances.'

'When was this?' asked Holmes.

'Just over a year ago,' he replied. 'But I couldn't find a proper job here as a pathologist, due to my past ... misdemeanours. I had to work yet again as an attendant in the mortuary at Barts, this time at night. I decided that a desperate situation demanded a desperate remedy. And so I developed a plan to kill my ex-wife and make it look like an accident. Then I would inherit her house, the same property that I had paid for, incidentally, *chaps*, with the first twenty years of my working life! I could sell it to finance a change of career in a country that was not so fussy about bloody documents.'

'What did you do to Mrs Hudson?' I demanded forcefully, pushing the barrel of my pistol against his neck.

His voice went up a notch.

'I had rented a cab and was working as a cabbie during the day to supplement my income. My idea was to watch out for her when she went shopping down the Kensington High Street, and run her down.'

'Run her down,' repeated Holmes in wonder.

'Yes. And my plan almost worked! A few days ago, I spotted an opportunity to implement it. I whipped up the horses into a frenzy as she crossed the road and steered them straight into that stubborn, carnivorous, overweight witch! She received a ferocious clout from a single hoof that sent her sprawling onto the pavement. I thought that I had succeeded, and was checking her out when I heard a policeman's whistle nearby. Panicking, I grabbed her handbag and ring and took off in my hansom like the devil himself.'

'But how do you know that she is in a coma at Barts?' I demanded. 'And why didn't the hospital inform us of the matter?'

'Yes,' added Holmes. 'Do tell, old sport. Why all this kidnapping malarkey and silly coded messages?'

Hudson shrank back into his chair.

'I hastened back here to take a breather and plan my next move. It didn't take long for me to realise that I had to find out if Martha was dead, or not. I knew that she would be moved to Barts, either way, so I decided to pay a visit to work in the middle of the day, just to collect something from the mortuary ... supposedly.'

'Supposedly?' queried Holmes.

'Yes. What I really did was check admissions at reception, who had no problem in showing a mortuary attendant that an unidentified middle-aged woman had come in an hour ago, in a coma. She had no papers on her, and noone knew who she was. That was when the first glimmerings of another plan started to form in my mind. What were the chances of the world's first consulting detective knowing the whereabouts of his housekeeper? I asked myself this question, and came up with the answer.'

'Very little,' suggested Holmes. 'Especially as you had her handbag and ring.'

'Yes! Exactly! And so the idea of a staged kidnapping entered my plan. I could not be sure of inheriting 221B Baker Street, but what if I could extract some extra profit before she either died or woke up? I had nothing to lose. I wrote the first ransom note in a way that might intrigue her tenant, and left it in the door of her home. Simple, but effective. I knew that I could harvest the necessary body parts that night when I started work at Barts.'

'Harvest?' I cried. 'Harvest? Sacrilege! That's what it is!'

Hudson continued in alarm, his face sheened with sweat as I pulled back the trigger on my gun. How I would have loved to blow his own head off right at that moment!

'Sure enough, a woman who would serve my purpose came in after an accident at an ice-rink. I extracted her from the freezer, where she awaited embalming and transferred her to my cab in the early hours of the morning. I knew that a smart tec' like you would not come up with the readies immediately, so I started to cut her up here and deliver them to you, one piece at a time. Her tongue was quite fresh, her hand sawed off easily, and you have seen the head, of course, Dr. Watson! Which would have been found by you at the roller in Lord's, with another coded message, looking for five thousand pounds! I was actually planning to get to ten thousand, until you pair of busybodies spoiled everything. But you dropped the catch!'

'Watson!' warned Holmes, who perceived my desire to provide a swift justice for Mrs Hudson, whether she recovered or not. He stood up abruptly and grabbed a table-cloth. 'Keep your pistol on this pathetic goon while I tie him up. We'll attach him to his friend in the bedroom. He will enjoy that. Then you wait here until I have informed Lestrade. If you want to find me afterwards, I shall be at the bedside of Mrs Hudson in Barts. You! Worm! Stand up! Hands behind your back!'

Holmes kept watch over his housekeeper for another three days, barely using the cot supplied to him by the hospital. That was when she woke up and asked him if he wanted a cup of tea. She soon recovered fully and acted as a witness at the trial of Morse Hudson for attempted murder and extortion. This testimony helped to put her ex-husband away for twenty years of hard labour. I paid a visit to 221B Baker Street shortly after her discharge from hospital, in order to wish her well, only to hear some rather disturbing news.

'I thought that you should be the first to know, old chap. I am planning to retire from all forms of criminal investigation soon. This will involve my leaving London for good, to settle somewhere in the country.'

'But where? And what will you do?'

'Sussex, perhaps. I intend to study the habits of bees, specifically the honey-bee, and write a textbook on the subject. It is my hope that Mrs Hudson, fully recovered and with all her body parts intact, will be joining me as my housekeeper. Perhaps you might visit us occasionally, with your charming wife ... Beatrice?'

'Oh, yes, indeed.'

I found it difficult to keep the disappointment from my voice. 'I wonder what is the level of crime down there?'

'Negligible. Except amongst bees, perhaps. But we never know what the future holds, do we?' smiled Holmes languidly.

'No. Perhaps not,' I replied, thinking hopefully of a previous hiatus that had resulted in his miraculous return from certain death at the Reichenbach Falls in Switzerland.

'Anything can happen. It will take me at least a year to organise this change of life. I must find a suitable property for purchase. It will be a lengthy process. I have to begin my apiary studies. And I suppose that Mrs Hudson will be arranging the rental of 221B Baker Street. I am sure a case or two will emerge during that period of time.'

'Let us hope so, and that they are worthy testimonials to the skills of the world's first consulting detective,' I added loyally, yet with more than a touch of sadness in my heart.

'Cheer up, old chap. Perhaps you would care to join Martha and myself now at Simpson's for some of that roast beef I did not manage to sample last night?'

'Yes. Of course, Holmes. Only too delighted. I shall send a telegram to inform Beatrice of my decision to eat out.'

16. Sherlock Holmes And The Undiscovered Country.

Tap. Tap. Tap.

Lady Conan Doyle began the séance in her customary manner, leaning forward over her message pad, pencil in eager hand, eyes closed tightly.

'Are you there, Pheneas?'

Silence, except for the soft plash of snow against the windowpanes. None of the other people holding hands around the table looked up. The medium's main spirit guide usually took some time to come through. He was a busy man.

Tap. Tap. Tap.

'I repeat. Are you there, Pheneas?'

The dining-room at Windlesham Manor was darkened by heavy curtains drawn across the single bay window. The only faint light on that late evening of Friday, January 6th, 1930, came from the ashes of a dying fire.

Sir Arthur Conan Doyle sat beside his wife and prayed inwardly for a good show. He desperately wanted his neighbour, Lord Worthington Forbray, a local judge, cynic and non-believer, who was far more scathing about spiritualism than his old friend Houdini, to experience these messages from the far side. Pheneas had been a scribe in the city of Ur, three thousand years before the birth of Christ, and was a very, very high soul indeed, who had been sent especially to work through Jean Conan Doyle upon the earth plane. Had not Pheneas made his son Kingsley appear to him a month after the poor lad's death, and kiss his father upon the forehead?

Suddenly the sensitive's breathing grew heavier, her eyelids fluttered wildly, the body trembled and her hand began to move. It gathered pace and was soon travelling at extraordinary speed across the pad, each sheet from the block being ripped off by her husband when it had filled up. As instructed, the other guests kept their heads down throughout the following ten minutes of intense scribbling, until Lady Doyle finally collapsed, utterly exhausted. She appeared to have fallen asleep.

The group separated, leaning back in their chairs and stretching their arms in relief. One elegant lady, Jacintha O'Brien, a close friend of the medium, stood up abruptly from the table, switched on the overhead lights and moved across to place a comforting arm around the shoulder of Lady Conan Doyle.

'She will come out of it soon,' grunted her husband, as he gathered together the slips of paper, and started to read them one at a time to the group, as though he himself was the messenger.

'*We have been waiting for you to sit, my most beloved brother. Time is short, and there are few channels for us to ... tell so much that is important. Don't lose an opportunity. I want to say ... this. A new world will arise – new in all ways. Then all the shadows ... and darkness of the present world will be extinct. If humanity knew how different the world can be. Waken up ... your sluggish minds. You are helping all the time. Everyone has their part to play. What a thing ... to live for! What a privilege! The veil will be rent, and all shall see their dear ... ones. It is essential that you should teach them that the dead are alive. When the great change comes ... to humanity then all creeds and churches will cease to exist, for the people of all nations will realise how ...*'

Sir Arthur broke off as a coughing fit left him purple in the face and spluttering into a handkerchief. Once he had recovered, he twirled his grizzled moustache, glanced apologetically around the group, and continued to read.

'... *they have utterly failed them in their hour of need. All, all, every colour and sect and nation will turn ... to spiritualism, and so the world will be changed, and the shams will be swept away for ever. Then comes the Millenium. ... When you come over here to the land of your dreams you will find that only love prevails, and the sun shines, and all, all, is beautiful, and the heart is never ... hurt. From here you will see the progress of the world under the new conditions. It will all be most ... interesting and wonderful to behold. The crop is nearly due, the seeds are almost all in, the rain is now to come, and ... then the sunshine. It is the greatest thing that could possibly happen for humanity. God bless you ... and your beloved soul's mate, your boys, your girls, all those you love, or who have ever been kind and loving to you.'*

Conan Doyle shuffled the papers together, placed them in his pocket and gazed enquiringly at Lord Forbray, who was in the process of snipping off the end of an Upmann Cuban cigar.

'Well?' he wheezed. 'What do you think, old chap?'

The whey-faced judge set fire to his tobacco and blew a thin stream of blue smoke across the table, before shaking his head in exasperation.

'My dear fellow, this is an excellent example of the *carpenter* effect. A simple ideo-motor action that results from your good wife's unconscious mind connecting to the muscular movement of her hand and fingers. I am certain she is not making these messages up, and that you are both sincere in your beliefs. And I am sorry for your losses. But I shall continue to hold that once we are dead, we are dead. And the dead cannot communicate with the living. Nor vice versa. It is just wishful thinking on your part. Pheneas or no Pheneas.'

'Damn it all, Forbray,' cried Doyle. 'There must be more to this world that mere rationality! Surely there is mystery! The unknown! I myself have felt the touch of a vanished hand. What do I have to do in order to convince you of the truth?'

Sir Arthur never discovered the answer to this question, as his wife leapt up suddenly, trance-like, eyes still firmly shut, arms held tight by her sides, and exclaimed in a sharp man's voice, one that seemed vaguely familiar to the world's most famous writer, 'Conan Doyle, Conan Doyle'.

An uncanny sense of foreboding struck the recipient of these words. His forehead broke into a sweat.

'I am here,' he said.

You see, but you do not observe. The distinction is clear.'

Conan Doyle stood up, wide-eyed, and glared at his wife.

'What! What? How can this be? Holmes? You do not exist! You are not real! This is not possible! You cannot be dead, because you have never lived!'

The medium ignored this outburst and continued in exactly the same tone.

'It is an old maxim of mine that when you have excluded the impossible, whatever remains, however improbable, must be the truth.'

Doyle slammed his fist onto the table and shouted, 'Rubbish! I made you up! What box of tricks is this?'

His wife droned on in the voice of the world's first consulting detective.

'It is a capital mistake to theorize before one has data.'

Snow fell through the chimney and caused the fire to spit a nugget of coal onto the carpet, singeing it.

'Stop it, Jean! Oh, stop it!'

'There is nothing more deceptive than an obvious fact.'

'Dear God! How could he ...? The vibrations are all wrong! Aaaarrrrgggghhhh.' Conan Doyle clutched his heart and fell heavily onto the floor.

The sensitive continued to speak as though nothing had happened.

'You know my method. It is founded upon the observation of trifles.'

'Dad. Dad. Are you okay?'

'It is my business to know what other people don't know.'

Adrian Conan Doyle pushed back his chair and rushed over to his father.

'The game is afoot!'

With this final utterance, Lady Conan Doyle collapsed back into her seat, looking to the rest of the table as though she had entered a coma.

'Can you help me get him up to bed?' asked Adrian of his brother Denis.

'It's just his Angina Pectoris,' Denis explained to the group. 'Our father has these periodic attacks. He needs to take one of his tablets and lie down for a while. You grab one arm and I'll take the other, Adrian. Jacintha, can you look after mother? Excuse us, ladies and gentlemen.'

The remaining five members of the meeting rose from the table as one. Lord Forbray and his bejewelled, terribly bored wife were delighted to depart the scene, having agreed to come only out of a sense of loyalty to a close neighbour. Neither of them believed for a second in the idea of spiritualism becoming the new 'psychic religion' that Conan Doyle was intent on establishing. The poor chap had obviously never recovered from the loss of his son in that war to end all wars. Twelve years ago! It really was time he got over it. And why would his wife play such a bad joke on him? Sherlock Holmes, indeed!

The other three women were disappointed, and somewhat less willing to leave. They were widows, and each one had hoped to receive a message from their late husbands, informing them that life in summerland was absolutely wonderful, full of butterflies, flowers, sunshine and happiness, and they should experience no guilt whatsoever at having outlived them. *'Darling dears, do enjoy spending our money until your own time comes to join us up here'* were the words they desperately wanted to hear.

But it was not to be.

The bees were gone. And the hives were falling apart. Oh, well. It was only to be expected. After all, he *had* been away for fifteen years or more. When Mycroft needed his help during the Great War, he had to leave them in the care of a nearby farmer, who had since died. They must have buzzed away to other hives, other queens.

Now, on his seventy-sixth birthday, and with both his elder brother and poor old Watson six feet under the sod, his return to Cuckmere Haven was filled with bittersweet memories of the peace to be found upon the Sussex Downs. Even in the heart of winter, with a snow blizzard beating against the shutters on the windows and doors.

Mind you, the cottage itself had become pretty dilapidated, and needed a thorough cleanout. Although the stove was still working, it would be necessary to get new furniture in every room. And that leaking roof had to be fixed, as well as the front windows.

First things first. Weather permitting, tomorrow he would take a stroll along the coastal path into Seaford, in search of a housekeeper. Someone local should fit the bill. No need for her to live in. He also needed to shop around for a few tools he was missing. And the right kind of wood. Then he could start his new life.

There was to be no more sleuthing. No more murders. No more disguises and silly puzzles. No more damsels in distress. No more investigations into stolen jewellery, thank heavens. No more missing wives (hardly a crime, although Watson might have disagreed), husbands, paintings, artifacts, letters or vitally important state documents. No more Jasper and Lily Lestrade and their squalling infants. Truth be told, the last few cases with Watson had not exhibited his unusual skills in anything like a shining light. One does grow old.

Never mind.

Lots of glorious hill walks along the downs to look forward to. Many books to read. New melodies to be created and played upon his Stradivarius. And perhaps an occasional shot of cocaine, to while away the boredom. Why not?

Bliss upon bliss.

Farewell, Sherlock Holmes, detective.

Hello, Sherlock Holmes.

Carpenter.

'What are you doing out of bed?' demanded Jean. 'You know the doctor recommended complete rest for at least a month. Otherwise that big, generous heart of yours will give up the ghost altogether. I've brought you some beef broth for lunch.'

Arthur sighed, turned away from the window and tumbled back into his four poster. His wife settled the tray across his legs.

'I just wanted to see if it had stopped snowing, that's all. And to hell with Doctor Barrie. Death holds no terror for a spiritualist. In fact, I'm quite looking forward to arguing with that sceptic Houdini again. But I'd still like to know what you were up to, introducing Sherlock Holmes like that last night.'

Ignoring his broth altogether, he picked up his briar and proceeded to stuff it with a wad of his favourite Arcadia ship's tobacco.

Jean sat down on the bed beside him, and reached over to caress his hand fondly.

'Arthur. You know very well that I am not in control of what happens to me when I enter a trance state. We cannot call up the dead. It is they who come to call on us. If Holmes really did arrive last night from the spirit world, then perhaps it is because you managed to conjure him up yourself. This character has haunted you all your life. He is your inner torment, my dearest one. And I am very sensitive to your vibrations. Now eat up your soup. Have you taken your tablet?'

Doyle sucked on his pipe to get it going and patted her hand back.

'Oh, you are wonderful. Yes, of course I have. But those words you spoke from your trance. They are straight out of my books. Anyone could know them off by heart. People pretend to be him and speak his lines in the street! *What you do in this world is a matter of no consequence. The question is what can you make people believe you have done.'* And this one has taken on an entirely new meaning: *'Is there any other point to which you would wish to draw my attention? To the curious incident of the dog in the night-time. The dog did nothing in the night-time. That was the curious incident.'* Blah, blah, blah. As though it had some deep philosophical meaning. Bloody Strand Magazine. When I think of the effort I put into writing my historical novels about Britain – *Rodney Stone, Sir Nigel, The White Company, Brigadier Gerard, et al*, as well as the Professor Challenger stories, I get thoroughly depressed at the degree of interest shown by the fickle public in those simple, harmless puzzles about everyday crimes. There was a time when I could write one of them in a day, as well as playing two rounds of golf. Pshaw!'

'Now don't you think about it any more, dear. You will only make yourself more agitated. Just remember the money that Sherlock has put in your pocket.'

Conan Doyle steadied his pipe on the tray and spooned up some broth.

'Aahh, that is good. You are right, as usual. We could not have afforded Windlesham without the world's first consulting detective. Nor the Psychic Bookshop, and our travels around the world to spread the gospel about spiritualism. Nevertheless, I wish I'd killed him off for good at the same time as Doctor Watson. Or left him to drown at the foot of the Reichenbach Falls, all those years ago. Do you know, last night I dreamed that Holmes was actually a real person, who was still living over in Cuckmere Haven. Ridiculous notion.'

He continued to sip his broth before mopping it up with a slice of bread. Then he took up his pipe again.

147

'Old Forbray wasn't buying into our demonstration, was he?'

Jean removed the tray and stood up from the bed.

'No. And his wife is not a believer, either. We must recognise that this new religion will take many years to establish itself in Britain. After all, it took decades after his death for Jesus to be recognised as the Son of God.'

'Yes. And centuries before Christianity spread to the far corners of the earth,' mused her husband. 'With all the disagreements and schisms it had to go through, I'm surprised it still exists at all. Yet I continue to believe in the Second Coming! Only those who believe shall be allowed to enter His glorious realm! Out of the mud! Out of the mire!'

His wife turned around at the door.

'Calm down and don't think about such things. Remember what Doctor Barrie said about stress and overwork. Your heart needs constant rest to increase its strength again. You have a nap now. I'll send Billie up later on. She's very concerned about her daddy. As we all are.'

When his wife had closed the door, Arthur Conan Doyle puffed away at his pipe and continued to contemplate the unsatisfactory results of the previous night's séance. It could have been anybody who was familiar with the canon, of course. They might have learnt off the popular phrases while they were still alive. Or even Joseph Bell himself, his inspiration for the character, who had passed on about twenty years ago. Yet surely his old lecturer would not have been bothered with the adventures of Sherlock Holmes?

It might have made more sense if the contact had been Watson. At least he was supposed to be dead.

But that voice! It was exactly how he imagined the great detective would speak.

If he had been a real person.

———————————

Once the table and chairs were finished, he'd start on a kitchen dresser. Not that he had many items to store in one, but Miss Olwen Rees, the new housekeeper he had employed a month ago, insisted on furniture that created some degree of order in the kitchen. A single stove was not enough for her domain.

Their arrangement was that she would come in every five days, clean out the fires, dust and sweep, take away any laundry for washing, and cook meals for him that would last for the next five days, heated up or cold.

But he had made a serious mistake. Not for the first time with the fair sex, as Watson would insist on calling them.

At the interview in Seaford, the plump middle-aged widow had shown no signs of being even more interfering than Mrs Hudson, and that she would be constantly enquiring as to whether he wanted a cup of tea, or not. Not, thank you! That was, of course, when she wasn't down on her blasted knees, praying to some long forgotten saint from her home town's Presbyterian Church in Llangollen.

Or even worse than that. What was it the Welsh did? They sang!

'Ah, cruel was my father that did my flight restrain,
And I was cruel-hearted that did at home remain,
With you, my love, contented, I'd journey far away;
Why, Owen, did you leave me? At home why did I stay?'

149

The carpenter gritted his teeth as he sawed away at a long pine plank. Patience, man! It was only a couple of hours every five days, and she had her own key. Once all the furniture was ready, and the fixtures working smoothly, he would be sure to take a long walk in advance of each arrival. And at least she had never heard of the world's first consulting detective, Sherlock Holmes, and wasn't blathering on non-stop about orange pips, speckled bands, dancing or crooked men and all those *wonderful* detective stories that Watson had cobbled together.

He really should be grateful for small mercies.

'I've been thinking about something. It has weighed heavily upon my mind. I want you to contact Holmes again. Just the two of us. Nobody else need be present. Except for Pheneas, of course.'

It had been several weeks since Conan Doyle's heart disease had brought on his chest pains at the séance. February 2nd was the midpoint of winter, and he had recovered sufficiently to celebrate that bright Candlemas Day with his family at the local Anglican Church. Now he was finishing off a late supper of haddock kedgeree with his wife, their three children having vanished to various parts of the house.

Jean Conan Doyle paused in the act of spooning some chutney onto her plate.

'I think that is a really bad idea, Arthur,' she sighed. 'Consider what happened the last time. Your health is not up to another shock. It was just an aberration. He probably won't appear again. Why on earth do you want to do this now?'

150

'Because I need to solve the mystery,' he replied. 'There must be *some* reason for his appearance. It could be Doctor Bell trying to get in touch with me, using those phrases from my books. Or someone else who needs my help. For what? We don't know. Yet.'

His wife's voice softened.

'Like Kingsley, for instance? You still miss him, don't you?'

'That *bloody* Spanish flu!' he exclaimed, with tears in his eyes. 'Having survived the Somme! My beloved son! It just wasn't fair!'

'Hush. Don't get all het up again. When we have finished our supper, I shall endeavour to contact Pheneas,' she replied patiently. 'But there will be no automatic writing. I am too tired for that. Just don't be disappointed if nothing happens, and noone comes through.'

Fifteen minutes later, Conan Doyle switched off the lights in the dining-room, and turned the key in the door.

'I don't want you to be disturbed by any alien forces,' he explained.

His wife stood up, spread her fingers out on the table and closed her eyes.

'Pheneas? Pheneas?'

Nothing. Absolute silence.

Tap. Tap. Tap.

'Pheneas?'

More silence, which lasted for several moments. Then:

'Conan Doyle? Conan Doyle?'

It was the same voice, spoken by his wife in that same rigid trance-like state. But could it really be his own creation, Sherlock Holmes, the world's first consulting detective?

'Yes. I am here.'

'I am Alpha and Omega, the beginning and the end, the first and the last.'

'What? Oh, my Good Lord. Jesus Christ.'

Conan Doyle fell to his knees upon the floor. His body froze in recognition of the quote from the Revelation of St. John The Divine. Could it be true? Had the time come? For the Rapture and seeing his son Kingsley and brother Innes in Heaven again? But why communicate the message through his wife like this? And in that voice?

'I Jesus have sent mine angel to testify unto you these things in the churches.'

Yes. Yes. Yes. Conan Doyle was ready. He clasped his hands together tightly. Ready to be reborn.

'I am the root and the offspring of David, and the bright and morning star.'

But what about Jean and their new family? Will they also be welcome? After all, he had loved her for ten years while his first wife was still alive, something he felt guilty about.

'Surely I come quickly.'

With this, his wife slumped down into her chair.

Her husband waited. Patiently. His mind had become a total blank and his knees trembled violently.

After about five minutes of this, he summoned the courage to peep between his fingers. There was noone there! No white light. No bright star, shining from the corner of the room. No beautiful bearded man, calling him up to paradise. Just Jean, coming out of her trance.

'What ... what happened?' she asked. 'What are you doing down there?'

Conan Doyle stood up slowly, his knees creaking. He avoided eye contact with his wife.

'Eh, I just wanted to say a short prayer.'

'To whom?'

'To the Lord our God. Did you not feel His power within you? His Son spoke to me through you. But with Sherlock's voice.'

'No. I did not. Now that *is* interesting. What did He say?'

Conan Doyle repeated the words of the spirit to his wife.

'Hhmm. Revelations,' she replied. 'Do sit down, Arthur. I'll send for a fresh pot of tea. Otherwise you will have another attack of angina. And Jesus Christ would not want that, now would he?'

Conan Doyle did as he was told. But his heart was pounding in his chest and his left foot had started a frantic Saint Vitus Dance.

'I suppose if Pheneas can communicate with us, it's only logical that someone born several thousand years later might be able to do the same,' he stated. 'Still, it's quite a shock. Especially that voice. I was sure it was Holmes.'

'Maybe it's just a warning of what is to come,' suggested Jean. 'You know. For us to be ready.'

Conan Doyle's innocent features brightened up.

'Yes, of course. That's it, by Jove! Well done, my sweet young girl. Salvation is at hand. He is on His way. We must be prepared for the great day. I shall write about this vision later on, and talk about it at the next meeting of the London Spiritual Alliance on Thursday. Now where's that tea?'

Oh, dear God. She was singing again. Some obscure Welsh hymn. Wasn't it called *Bread Of Heaven* in English? Watson would have loved it.

He had to get away. Even though there was a bed to be made and he was tired of sleeping on the floor upstairs.

A long walk was called for. There was a map somewhere. Not along the coast. He would head inland for a change, towards Crowborough. Across the hills and over the dales. It was about twenty-four miles, so he could stay overnight in Sandy Cross, and take a train back from Crowborough to Seafield on the morrow.

What day was it? His calendar read the fourteenth of March, and a fine spring one to boot, with a slight breeze wafting through a clear Cambridge blue sky. Ten minutes to pack, and then it would be time to bid farewell to the lilting tones of Miss Olwen Rees.

Only temporarily.

Unfortunately.

––––––––––––––

This was the day he went out to pick the flower.

Every year since their meeting, Conan Doyle had plucked the first snowdrop of the season on the fifteenth of March. He had met his beloved second wife on that date in 1897, and he was determined to recognise the anniversary this year, even though he had been confined to bed by his doctor.

The appearance of his saviour at the last séance had placed him in a bad way. He had difficulty breathing and needed regular doses of oxygen to steady his heart.

Nevertheless he had managed to sneak down the stairs while his family were at lunch, through the hall and out into the front garden, without being noticed by anyone.

What a glorious day!

What a singular triumph it was to be alive!

Sherlock Holmes breathed the sharp spring air deeply into his lungs. It mixed well with the black shag tobacco from his pipe. He had managed to walk a sterling fifteen miles the previous day, and yet he felt twenty years younger, after a night's perfect sleep in The Sheep's Head Tavern in Sandy Cross.

What a fine-looking house that was! And a striking-looking chap too, doing some early season gardening.

Great heavens! He looked a bit like Watson.

'Good day to you, old fellow,' he chirped, waving his pipe at the gentleman as he passed by on his way to Crowborough.

'Aaaarrrrgggghhhh'!

Editor's Postscript:

It is not known whether the sight of a tall, thin, hawk-nosed, gangling frame of a fellow, puffing away on a clay pipe, wearing neither deerstalker hat nor Inverness cape, but strolling nonchalantly along the path in front of Windlesham House, caused the heart attack that was to end the great writer's life several months later.

But Arthur Conan Doyle *was* found that same day in his front garden, lying on the ground, clutching his heart with one hand, while his other held a single white snowdrop.

And after all, Sherlock Holmes was not a living human being, but merely a figment of the famous writer's imagination.

Wasn't he?

Editor's Post-postscript:

Quite how this manuscript found its way into a cabinet in the basement of 221B Baker Street, where it lay undiscovered until 1955, and who wrote it, is anybody's guess.

Perhaps there were supernatural forces at work.

Also from MX Publishing

MX Publishing is the world's largest specialist Sherlock Holmes publisher, with over a hundred titles and fifty authors creating the latest in Sherlock Holmes fiction and non-fiction.

From traditional short stories and novels to travel guides and quiz books, MX Publishing cater for all Holmes fans.

The collection includes leading titles such as *Benedict Cumberbatch In Transition* and *The Norwood Author* which won the 2011 Howlett Award (Sherlock Holmes Book of the Year).

MX Publishing also has one of the largest communities of Holmes fans on Facebook with regular contributions from dozens of authors.

www.mxpublishing.com

Also from MX Publishing

Our bestselling books are our short story collections;

'Lost Stories of Sherlock Holmes' , 'The Outstanding Mysteries of Sherlock Holmes', The Papers of Sherlock Holmes Volume 1 and 2, 'Untold Adventures of Sherlock Holmes' (and the sequel 'Studies in Legacy) and 'Sherlock Holmes in Pursuit', 'The Cotswold Werewolf and Other Stories of Sherlock Holmes' – and many more……

Also from MX Publishing

"Phil Growick's, 'The Secret Journal of Dr Watson', is an adventure which takes place in the latter part of Holmes and Watson's lives. They are entrusted by HM Government (although not officially) and the King no less to undertake a rescue mission to save the Romanovs, Russia's Royal family from a grisly end at the hand of the Bolsheviks. There is a wealth of detail in the story but not so much as would detract us from the enjoyment of the story. Espionage, counter-espionage, the ace of spies himself, double-agents, double-crossers...all these flit across the pages in a realistic and exciting way. All the characters are extremely well-drawn and Mr Growick, most importantly, does not falter with a very good ear for Holmesian dialogue indeed. Highly recommended. A five-star effort."
The Baker Street Society

www.mxpublishing.com

Also from MX Publishing

The Missing Authors Series

Sherlock Holmes and The
Adventure of The Grinning Cat
Sherlock Holmes and The Nautilus Adventure
Sherlock Holmes and The Round Table Adventure

"Joseph Svec, III is brilliant in entwining two endearing and enduring classics of literature, blending the factual with the fantastical; the playful with the pensive; and the mischievous with the mysterious. We shall, all of us young and old, benefit with a cup of tea, a tranquil afternoon, and a copy of Sherlock Holmes, The Adventure of the Grinning Cat."
Amador County Holmes Hounds Sherlockian Society

www.mxpublishing.com

Also from MX Publishing

The American Literati Series

The Final Page of Baker Street
The Baron of Brede Place
Seventeen Minutes To Baker Street

"The really amazing thing about this book is the author's ability to call up the 'essence' of both the Baker Street 'digs' of Holmes and Watson as well as that of the 'mean streets' of Marlowe's Los Angeles. Although none of the action takes place in either place, Holmes and Watson share a sense of camaraderie and self-confidence in facing threats and problems that also pervades many of the later tales in the Canon. Following their conversations and banter is a return to Edwardian England and its certainties and hope for the future. This is definitely the world before The Great War."
Philip K Jones

Also from MX Publishing

The Detective and The Woman Series

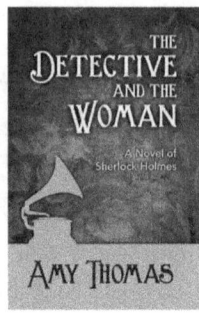  

The Detective and The Woman
The Detective, The Woman and The Winking Tree
The Detective, The Woman and The Silent Hive

"The book is entertaining, puzzling and a lot of fun. I believe the author has hit on the only type of long-term relationship possible for Sherlock Holmes and Irene Adler. The details of the narrative only add force to the romantic defects we expect in both of them and their growth and development are truly marvelous to watch. This is not a love story. Instead, it is a coming-of-age tale starring two of our favorite characters."
Philip K Jones

www.mxpublishing.com

Also from MX Publishing

The Sherlock Holmes and Enoch Hale Series

The Amateur Executioner
The Poisoned Penman
The Egyptian Curse

"The Amateur Executioner: Enoch Hale Meets Sherlock Holmes", the first collaboration between Dan Andriacco and Kieran McMullen, concerns the possibility of a Fenian attack in London. Hale, a native Bostonian, is a reporter for London's Central News Syndicate - where, in 1920, Horace Harker is still a familiar figure, though far from revered. "The Amateur Executioner" takes us into an ambiguous and murky world where right and wrong aren't always distinguishable. I look forward to reading more about Enoch Hale."
Sherlock Holmes Society of London

www.mxpublishing.com

Also from MX Publishing

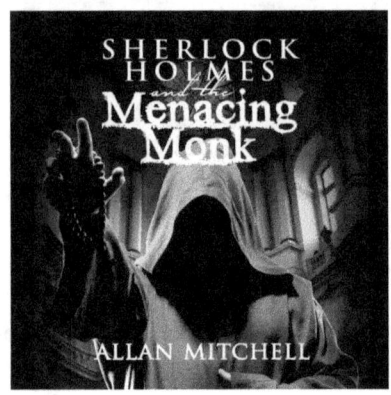

All four novellas have been released also in audio format with narration by Steve White

Sherlock Holmes and The Menacing Moors
Sherlock Holmes and The Menacing Metropolis
Sherlock Holmes and The Menacing Melbournian
Sherlock Holmes and The Menacing Monk

"The story is really good and the Herculean effort it must have been to write it all in verse—well, my hat is off to you, Mr. Allan Mitchell! I wouldn't dream of seeing such work get less than five plus stars from me…"
The Raven

Also from MX Publishing

When the papal apartments are burgled in 1901, Sherlock Holmes is summoned to Rome by Pope Leo XII. After learning from the pontiff that several priceless cameos that could prove compromising to the church, and perhaps determine the future of the newly unified Italy, have been stolen, Holmes is asked to recover them. In a parallel story, Michelangelo, the toast of Rome in 1501 after the unveiling of his Pieta, is commissioned by Pope Alexander VI, the last of the Borgia pontiffs, with creating the cameos that will bedevil Holmes and the papacy four centuries later. For fans of Conan Doyle's immortal detective, the game is always afoot. However, the great detective has never encountered an adversary quite like the one with whom he crosses swords in "The Vatican Cameos.."

"An extravagantly imagined and beautifully written Holmes story" (Lee Child, NY Times Bestseller, Jack Reacher series)

www.ingramcontent.com/pod-product-compliance
Lightning Source LLC
Chambersburg PA
CBHW051521170626
46811CB00002B/933

* 9 7 8 1 7 8 7 0 5 1 4 7 8 *